✔ KU-289-532

WITHDRAWN FROM STOCK
DUBLIN CITY PUBLIC LIBRARIES

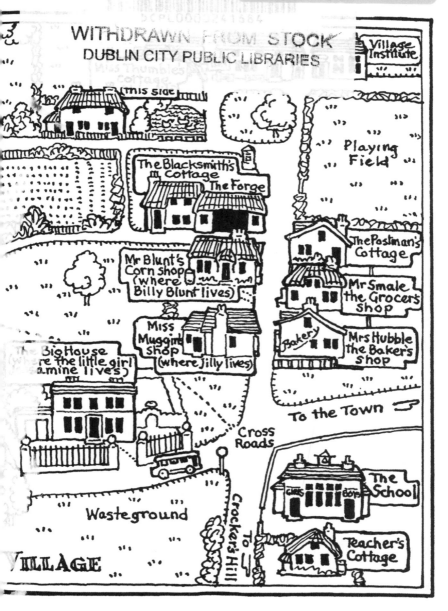

Village Institute

[This side]

The Blacksmith's Cottage
The Forge

Playing Field

The Postman's Cottage

Mr Blunt's Corn shop (where Billy Blunt lives)

Mr Smale the Grocer's shop

Miss Muggins shop (where Jilly lives)

Bakery

Mrs Hubble the Baker's shop

The Big House (where the little girl Jamine lives)

To the Town

Cross Roads

To Crockers Hill

Wasteground

GIRLS   BOYS

The School

Teacher's Cottage

VILLAGE

MORE MILLY-MOLLY-MOLLY-MANDY

This collection first published 1997 by Kingfisher

This edition published 2009 by Macmillan Children's Books
a division of Macmillan Publishers Limited
20 New Wharf Road, London N1 9RR
Basingstoke and Oxford
Associated companies throughout the world
www.panmacmillan.com

ISBN 978-0-230-74381-6

The stories in this collection first appeared in:
More of Milly-Molly-Mandy (1929)
Further Doings of Milly-Molly-Mandy (1932)
Milly-Molly-Mandy Again (1948)
Milly-Molly-Mandy & Co. (1955)
Milly-Molly-Mandy and Billy Blunt (1967)
Published by George G. Harrap & Co. Limited

Text and illustrations copyright © Joyce Lankester Brisley 1929, 1932, 1948, 1955, 1967

All rights reserved. No part of this publication may be
reproduced, stored in or introduced into a retrieval system, or
transmitted, in any form or by any means (electronic, mechanical,
photocopying, recording or otherwise), without the prior written
permission of the publisher. Any person who does any unauthorized
act in relation to this publication may be liable to criminal
prosecution and civil claims for damages.

1 3 5 7 9 8 6 4 2

A CIP catalogue record for this book is available from the British Library.

Printed and bound in the UK by CPI Mackays, Chatham ME5 8TD

This book is sold subject to the condition that it shall not,
by way of trade or otherwise, be lent, resold, hired out,
or otherwise circulated without the publisher's prior consent
in any form of binding or cover other than that in which
it is published and without a similar condition including this
condition being imposed on the subsequent purchaser.

MORE MILLY-MOLLY-MOLLY-MANDY

MACMILLAN CHILDREN'S BOOKS

CONTENTS

1

MILLY-MOLLY-MANDY
WRITES LETTERS

Once upon a time Milly-Molly-Mandy
heard the postman's knock, bang-BANG! on
the front door; so she ran hop-skip down the
passage to look in the
letter-box, because
she always sort of
hoped there might
be a letter for her!

But there wasn't.

"I do wish the post-
man would bring me a
letter sometimes," said
Milly-Molly-Mandy,
coming slowly back
into the kitchen. "He
never does. There's

Leabharlanna Poibli Chathair Bhaile Átha Cliath
Dublin City Public Libraries

only a business-looking letter
for Father and an advertise-
ment for Uncle."

And then Milly-Molly-Mandy
noticed that the business-looking
letter was from Holland (where
Father got his flower bulbs) and
had a Dutch stamp on it, so that was more
interesting. Milly-Molly-Mandy was collecting
foreign stamps. She had collected one Irish
one already, and it was stuck in Billy Blunt's
new stamp album. (Billy Blunt had just started
collecting stamps, so Milly-Molly-Mandy was
collecting for him.)

"If you want the postman to bring you letters
you'll have to write them to other people first,"
said Mother, putting the letters upon the mantelshelf till Father and Uncle should come in.

"But I haven't got any stamps," said Milly-
Molly-Mandy.

"I'll give you one when you want it," said
Grandma, pulling the kettle forward on the
stove.

"But I don't know who to write to," said
Milly-Molly-Mandy.

"You'll have to think round a little," said Aunty, clearing her sewing off the table.

"There's only Billy Blunt and little-friend-Susan, and it would be silly to write to them when I see them every day," said Milly-Molly-Mandy.

"We must just think," said Mother, spreading the cloth on the table for tea. "There are sure to be lots of people who would like to have letters by post, as well as you."

Milly-Molly-Mandy hadn't thought of that. "Do you suppose they'd run like anything to the letter-box because they thought there might be a letter from me?" she said. "What fun! I've got the fancy notepaper that Aunty gave me at Christmas – they'll like that, won't they? Who *can* I write to?"

And then she helped to lay the table, and made a piece of toast at the fire for Grandma; and presently Father and Uncle and Grandpa came in to tea, and Milly-Molly-Mandy was given the Dutch stamp off Father's letter. She put it in her pencil-box, ready for Billy Blunt in the morning.

And then she had an idea. "If I could write

to someone not in England they'd stick foreign stamps on their letters when they wrote back, wouldn't they?"

And then Aunty had an idea. "Why, there are my little nieces in America!" she said. (For Aunty had a brother who went to America when he was quite young, and now he had three little children, whom none of them had seen or knew hardly anything about, for "Tom", as Aunty called him, wasn't a very good letter writer, and only wrote to her sometimes at Christmas.)

"Ooh, yes!" said Milly-Molly-Mandy, "and I don't believe Billy has an American stamp yet. What are their names, Aunty? I forget."

"Sallie and Lallie," said Aunty, "and the boy is Tom, after my brother, but they call him Buddy. They would like to have a letter from their cousin in England, I'm sure."

So Milly-Molly-Mandy looked out the box of fancy notepaper that Aunty had given her, and kept it by her side while she did her home-lessons after tea. And then, when she had done them all, she wrote quite a long letter to her cousin Sallie (at least it looked quite a long letter, because the pink notepaper was rather small), telling about her school, and her friends, and Billy Blunt's collection, and about Toby the dog, and Topsy the cat, and what Father and Mother and Grandpa and Grandma and Uncle and Aunty were all doing at that moment in the kitchen, and outside in the barn; so that Sallie should get to know them all. And then there was just room to send her love to Lallie and Buddy, and to sign her name.

It was quite a nice letter.

Milly-Molly-Mandy showed it to Mother and Aunty, and then (just to make it more interesting) she put in a piece of coloured silver paper and two primroses (the first she had found that year), and stuck down the flap of the pink envelope.

The next morning she posted her letter in the red pillar-box on the way to school (little-

11

friend-Susan was quite interested when she showed her the address); and then she tried to forget all about it, because she knew it would take a long while to get there and a longer while still for an answering letter to come back.

After morning school she gave the Dutch stamp to Billy Blunt for his collection. He said he had got one, as they were quite common, but that it might come in useful for exchanging with some other fellow. And after school that very afternoon he told her he had exchanged it for a German stamp; so it was very useful.

"Have you got an American stamp?" asked Milly-Molly-Mandy.

"No," said Billy Blunt. "What I want to get hold of is a Czechoslovakian one. Ted Smale's just got one. His uncle gave it to him."

Milly-Molly-Mandy didn't think she could ever collect such a stamp as that for Billy Blunt, but she was glad he hadn't got an American one yet.

All that week and the next Milly-Molly-Mandy rushed to the letter-box every time she

heard the postman, although she knew there
wouldn't be an answer for about three weeks,
anyhow. But the postman's knock, bang-
BANG! sounded so exciting she always forgot
to remember in time.

A whole month went by, and Milly-Molly-
Mandy began almost to stop expecting a letter
at all, or at least one from abroad.

And then one day she came
home after school a bit later
than usual, because she
and little-friend-Susan
had been picking wind-
flowers and primroses
under a hedge, very excited to think spring had
really come. But when she
did get in what DO you think she found waiting for her, on her plate at the table?

Why, *three* letters, just come by post! One
from Sallie, one from Lallie, and one from
Buddy!

They were so pleased at having a letter from
England that they had all written back, hoping she would write again. And they sent some

They sat and wrote letters together

snapshots of themselves, and Buddy enclosed a Japanese stamp for Billy Blunt's collection.

The next Saturday Billy Blunt came to tea with Milly-Molly-Mandy and she gave him the four stamps, three American and one Japanese. And, though he said they were not really valuable ones, he was pleased as anything to have them!

And when the table was cleared they sat and wrote letters together – Milly-Molly-Mandy to Sallie and Lallie, and Billy Blunt to Buddy (to thank him for the stamp), with a little P.S. from Milly-Molly-Mandy (to thank him for his letter).

Milly-Molly-Mandy does like letter-writing, because now she has got three more friends!

2

MILLY-MOLLY-MANDY
CAMPS OUT

ONCE UPON A TIME Milly-Molly-Mandy and Toby the dog went down to the village, to Miss Muggins's shop, on an errand for Mother; and as they passed Mr Blunt's corn-shop Milly-Molly-Mandy saw something new in the little garden at the side. It looked like a small, shabby sort of tent, with a slit in the top and a big checked patch sewn on the side.

Milly-Molly-Mandy wondered what it was doing there. But she didn't see Billy Blunt anywhere about, so she couldn't ask him.

When she came out of Miss Muggins's shop she had another good look over the palings into the Blunts's garden. And while she was looking Billy Blunt came out of their house door with some old rugs and a pillow in his arms.

16

"Hullo, Billy!" said Milly-Molly-Mandy. "What's that tent-thing?"

"It's a tent," said Billy Blunt, not liking its being called "thing".

"But what's it for?" asked Milly-Molly-Mandy.

"It's mine," said Billy Blunt.

"Yours? Your very own? Is it?" said Milly-Molly-Mandy. "Ooh, do let me come and look at it!"

"You can if you want to," said Billy Blunt. "I'm going to sleep in it tonight – camp out."

Milly-Molly-Mandy was very interested indeed. She looked at it well, out-side and in. She could only just stand up in it. Billy Blunt had spread an old mackintosh for a ground sheet, and there was a box in one corner to hold a bottle of water and a mug, and his electric torch, and such necessary things; and when the front flap of the

17

tent was closed you couldn't see anything outside, except a tiny bit of sky and some green leaves through the tear in the top.

Milly-Molly-Mandy didn't want to come out a bit, but Billy Blunt wanted to put his bedding in.

"Isn't it beautiful! Where did you get it, Billy?" she asked.

"My cousin gave it to me," said Billy Blunt. "Used it when he went cycling holidays. He's got a new one now. I put that patch on, myself."

Milly-Molly-Mandy thought she could have done it better; but still it was quite good for a boy, so she duly admired it, and offered to mend the other place. But Billy Blunt didn't think it was worth it, as it would only tear away again – and he liked a bit of air, anyhow.

"Shan't you feel funny out here all by yourself when everybody else is asleep?" said Milly-Molly-Mandy. "Oh, I wish I had a tent too!" Then she said goodbye, and ran with Toby the dog back home to the nice white cottage with the thatched roof, thinking of the tent all the way.

She didn't see little-friend-Susan as she passed the Moggs's cottage along the road; but when she got as far as the meadow she saw her swinging her baby sister on the big gate.

"Hullo, Milly-Molly-Mandy! I was just looking for you," said little-friend-Susan, lifting Baby Moggs down. And Milly-Molly-Mandy told her all about Billy Blunt's new tent, and how he was going to sleep out, and how she wished she had a tent too.

Little-friend-Susan was almost as interested as Milly-Molly-Mandy. "Can't we make a tent and play in it in your meadow?" she said. "It would be awful fun!"

So they got some bean poles and bits of sacking from the barn and dragged them down into the meadow. And they had great fun that day trying to make a tent; only they couldn't get it to stay up properly.

Next morning little-friend-Susan came to play "tents" in the meadow again. And this time they tried with an old counterpane, which Mother had given them, and two kitchen chairs; and they managed to rig up quite a good tent by laying the poles across the

chair-backs and draping the counterpane over.
They fastened down the spread-out sides with
stones; and the ends, where the chairs were,
they hung with sacks. And there they had a
perfectly good tent, really quite big enough for
two – so long as the two were small, and didn't
mind being a bit crowded!

They were just sitting in it, eating apples
and pretending they had no other home to live
in, when they heard a "*Hi!*"-ing from the gate;
and when they peeped out there was Billy
Blunt, with a great bundle in his arms, trying
to get the gate open. So they ran across the
grass and opened it for him.

"What have you got? Is it your tent? Did you sleep out last night?" asked Milly-Molly-Mandy.

"Look here," said Billy Blunt, "do you think your father would mind, supposing I pitched my tent in your field? My folk don't like it in our garden – say it looks too untidy."

Milly-Molly-Mandy was quite sure Father wouldn't mind. So Billy Blunt put the bundle down inside the gate and went off to ask (for of course you never camp anywhere without saying "please" to the owner first). And Father didn't mind a bit, so long as no papers or other rubbish were left about.

So Billy Blunt set up his tent near the others', which was not too far from the nice white cottage with the thatched roof (because it's funny what a long way off from everybody you feel when you've got only a tent round you at night!). And then he went home to fetch his other goods; and Milly-Molly-Mandy and little-friend-Susan sat in his tent, and wished and wished that their mothers would let them sleep out in the meadow that night.

When Billy Blunt came back with his rugs

and things (loaded up on his box on wheels) they asked him if it were a very creepy-feeling to sleep out of doors.

And Billy Blunt (having slept out once) said, "Oh, you soon get used to it," and asked why they didn't try it in their tent.

So then Milly-Molly-Mandy and little-friend-Susan looked at each other, and said firmly, "Let's ask!" So little-friend-Susan went with Milly-Molly-Mandy up to the nice white cottage with the thatched roof, where Mother was just putting a treacle-tart into the oven.

She looked very doubtful when Milly-Molly-Mandy told her what they wanted to do. Then she shut the oven door, and wiped her hands, and said, well, she would just come and look at the tent they had made first. And when she had looked and considered, she said, well, if it were still very fine and dry by the evening perhaps Milly-Molly-Mandy might sleep out there, just for once. And Mother found a rubber ground-sheet and some old blankets and cushions, and gave them to her.

Then Milly-Molly-Mandy went with little-friend-Susan to the Moggs's cottage, where

Mrs Moggs was just putting their potatoes on to boil.

She looked very doubtful at first; and then she said, well, if Milly-Molly-Mandy's mother had been out to see, and thought it was all right, and if it were a *very* nice, fine evening, perhaps little-friend-Susan might sleep out, just for once.

So all the rest of that day the three were very busy, making preparations and watching the sky. And when they all went home for supper the evening was beautifully still and warm, and without a single cloud.

So, after supper, they all met together again in the meadow, in the sunset. And they shut and tied up the meadow gate. (It was all terribly exciting!)

23

They little feared Susan and Billy. They were wounded, yet

And Mother came out, with Father and Grandpa and Grandma and Uncle and Aunty, to see that all was right, and their ground-sheets well spread under their bedding.

Then Milly-Molly-Mandy and little-friend-Susan crawled into their tent, and Billy Blunt crawled into his tent. And presently Milly-Molly-Mandy crawled out again in her pyjamas, and ran about with bare feet on the grass with Toby the dog; and then little-friend-Susan and Billy Blunt, in their pyjamas, crawled out and ran about too (because it feels so very nice, and so sort of new, to be running about under the sky in your pyjamas!).

And Father and Mother and Grandpa and Grandma and Uncle and Aunty laughed, and looked on as if they wouldn't mind doing it too, if they weren't so grown up.

Then Mother said, "Now I think it's time you campers popped into bed. Goodnight!" And they went off home.

So Milly-Molly-Mandy and little-friend-Susan called "Goodnight!" and crawled into one tent, and Billy Blunt caught Toby the dog and crawled into the other.

And the trees outside grew slowly blacker and blacker until they couldn't be seen at all; and the owls hooted; and a far-away cow moo-ed; and now and then Toby the dog wuffed, because he thought he heard a rabbit; and sometimes Milly-Molly-Mandy or little-friend-Susan squeaked, because they thought they felt a spider walking on them. And once Billy Blunt called out to ask if they were still awake, and they said they were, and was he? and he said of course he was.

And then at last they all fell fast asleep.

And in no time at all the sun was shining through their tents, telling them to wake up and come out, because it was the next day.

And Billy Blunt and Milly-Molly-Mandy and little-friend-Susan DID enjoy that camping-out night!

3

MILLY-MOLLY-MANDY
FINDS A TRAIN

ONCE UPON A TIME Milly-Molly-Mandy
was playing with Billy Blunt down by the little
brook (which, you know, ran through the
fields at the back of the nice white cottage
with the thatched roof where Milly-Molly-
Mandy lived).

They had got their shoes and socks off, and
were paddling about in the water, and poking
about among the stones and moss, and enjoying themselves very much. Only it was so
interesting just about where their feet were
that they might have missed seeing something
else interesting, a little farther off, if a woodpecker hadn't suddenly started pecking in an
old tree near by, and made Billy Blunt look up.

He didn't see the woodpecker, but he did see
the something else.

"I say – what's that, there?" said Billy Blunt, standing up and staring.

"What's what, where?" said Milly-Molly-Mandy, standing up and staring too.

"There," said Billy Blunt, pointing.

And Milly-Molly-Mandy looked there. And she saw, in the meadow on the farther side of the brook, what looked like a railway train. Only there was no railway near the meadow.

"It looks like a train," said Milly-Molly-Mandy.

"Um-m," said Billy Blunt.

"But how did it get there?" said Milly-Molly-Mandy.

"Must have been pulled there," said Billy Blunt.

"But what for? Who put it there? When did it come?" said Milly-Molly-Mandy.

Billy Blunt didn't answer. He splashed back to get his boots and socks, and he splashed across the brook with them, and sat on the grass on the other side, and began to dab his feet with his handkerchief. So Milly-Molly-Mandy splashed across with her shoes and began to put them on too. And with her toes scrunched up in the shoes (because they were still damp and wouldn't straighten out at first) she ran and hopped after Billy Blunt, up the little bank and across the grass to the train.

They walked all round it, staring hard. It hadn't got an engine, or a guard's van. It was just a railway carriage, and it stood with its big iron wheels in the grass, looking odd and out-of-place among the daisies and butter-cups.

"It's like a funny sort of house," said Milly-Molly-Mandy, climbing up to peep in the win-dows. "I wish we could play in it. Look – that could be the kitchen, and that's the sitting-room, and that's the bedroom. I wish we could get in!"

It had several doors either side, each with a big 3 painted on. Billy Blunt tried the handles in turn. They all seemed to be locked. But the last one wasn't! It opened heavily, and they could get into one compartment.

29

"It's old," said Billy Blunt, looking about. "I expect they've thrown it away."

"What a waste!" said Milly-Molly-Mandy. "Well, it's ours now. We found it. We can live in it, and go journeys!"

It was very exciting. They shut the door and they opened the windows. And then they sat down on the two wooden seats, and pretended they were going away for a holiday. When they stood up, or walked to the windows to look out, it was difficult to do it steadily, because the train rushed along so fast! Once it let out a great long whistle, so that Milly-Molly-Mandy jumped; and Billy Blunt grinned and did it again.

"We are just going through a station," he explained.

The next moment Milly-Molly-Mandy nearly fell over and knocked Billy Blunt.

"We've stopped suddenly – the signal must be up," she explained. So they each hung out of a window to look. "Now it's down and we're going on again," said Milly-Molly-Mandy.

"We're going into a tunnel now," said Billy

Blunt, pulling up his window by the strap. So Milly-Molly-Mandy pulled up hers – to keep the smoke out!

When the train stopped at last they got out, and everything looked quite different all round. They were by the sea, and the train was a house. One of the seats was a table, and they laid Billy Blunt's damp handkerchief on it as a tablecloth, and put a rusty tin filled with buttercups in the middle.

But after a while Billy Blunt began to feel hungry, and then, of course, they knew it must be time to think of going home. So at last they shut the door of their wonderful train-house, and planned to meet there again as early as possible the next day.

And then they jumped back over the brook, and Billy Blunt went one way across the field, to his home by the corn-shop; and Milly-Molly-Mandy went the other way across the field, to the nice white cottage with the thatched roof, where she found Father and Mother and Grandpa and Grandma and Uncle and Aunty just ready to sit down to table.

The next day Milly-Molly-Mandy hurried to get all her jobs done – helping to wash up the breakfast things, and make the beds, and do the dusting. And as soon as she was free to play she ran straight out and down to the brook.

Billy Blunt was just coming across the field from the village, so she waited for him, and together they crossed over the brook, planning where they would go for their travels today.

"There it is!" said Milly-Molly-Mandy, almost as if she had expected the train to have run away in the night.

And then she stopped. And Billy Blunt stopped too.

There was a man with a cap on, sitting on the roof of the train, fixing up a sort of chimney. And there was a woman with an apron on, sweeping dust out of one of the doorways. And there was a baby in a shabby old pram near by, squealing. And there was a little dog, guarding a hand-cart piled with boxes and bundles, who barked when he saw Milly-Molly-Mandy and Billy Blunt.

"They've got our train!" said Milly-Molly-Mandy, staring.

"'Spect it's their train, really," said Billy Blunt.

Milly-Molly-Mandy edged a little nearer and spoke to the little dog, who got under the cart and barked again (but he wagged his tail at the same time). The woman in the apron looked up and saw them.

Milly-Molly-Mandy said, "Good morning. Is this your train?"

"Yes, it is," said the woman, knocking dust out of the broom.

"Are you going to live in it?" asked Milly-Molly-Mandy.

"Yes, we are," said the woman. "Bought and paid for it, we did, and got it towed here, and it's going to be our home now."

"Is this your baby?" asked Billy Blunt, jiggling the pram gently. The baby stopped crying and stared up at him. "What's its name?"

The woman smiled then. "His name is Thomas Thomas, like his father's," she said. "So it don't matter whether you call either of 'em by surname or given-name, it's all one."

Just then the man on the roof dropped his hammer down into the grass, and called out. "Here, mate, just chuck that up, will you?"

So Billy Blunt threw the hammer up, and the man caught it and went on fixing the chimney, while Billy Blunt watched and handed up other things as they were wanted. And the man told him that this end of the carriage was going to be the kitchen (just as Milly-Molly-Mandy had planned!), and the wall between it and the next compartment was to be taken away so as to make it bigger. The other end was the bedroom, with the long seats for beds.

Milly-Molly-Mandy stayed jiggling the pram to keep the baby quiet, and making friends with the little dog. And the woman told her she had got some stuff for window-curtains in the hand-cart there; and that they planned to make a bit of a garden round, to grow potatoes and cabbages in, so the house would soon look more proper. She said her husband was a tinker, and he hoped to get work mending pots and kettles in the villages near, instead of tramping about the country looking for it, as they had been doing.

She asked Milly-Molly-Mandy if she didn't think the baby would have quite a nice home, after a bit? And Milly-Molly-Mandy said she DID!

Presently the woman brought out from the hand-cart a frying-pan, and a newspaper parcel of sausages, and a kettle (which Milly-Molly-Mandy filled for her at the brook). So then Milly-Molly-Mandy and Billy Blunt knew it was time to be going.

They said goodbye to the man and woman, and stroked the little dog. (The baby was asleep.) And as they were crossing back over the brook the man called after them:

"If you've got any pots, pans, and kettles to mend, you know where to come to find Thomas Tinker!"

So after that Milly-Molly-Mandy and Billy

Blunt were always on the look-out for anyone who had a saucepan, frying-pan, or kettle which leaked or had a loose handle, and offered at once to take it to Thomas Tinker's to be mended. And people were very pleased, because Thomas Tinker mended small things quicker than Mr Rudge the blacksmith did, not being so busy making horse-shoes and mending ploughs and big things. Thomas Tinker and his wife were very grateful to Milly-Molly-Mandy and Billy Blunt.

But as Milly-Molly-Mandy said, "If we can get them plenty of work then they can go on living here. And if we can't have that train for ourselves I like next best for Mr Tinker and Mrs Tinker and Baby Tinker to have it – don't you, Billy?"

And Billy Blunt did.

4

MILLY-MOLLY-MANDY
AND DUM-DUM

ONCE UPON A TIME Milly-Molly-Mandy was wandering past the Big House down by the crossroads where the little girl Jessamine, and her mother, Mrs Green, lived (only they were away just now).

There was always a lot of flowers in the garden of the Big House, so it was nice to peep through the gate when you passed. Besides, Mr Moggs, little-friend-Susan's father, worked there (he was the gardener), and Milly-Molly-Mandy could see him now, weeding with a long-handled hoe.

"Hello, Mr Moggs," Milly-Molly-Mandy called through the gate (softly, because you don't like to shout in other people's gardens, even when you know the people are away). "Could I come in, do you think?"

Mr Moggs looked up and said, "Well, now, I shouldn't wonder but that you could!"

So Milly-Molly-Mandy pushed open the big iron gate and slipped through.

"Isn't it pretty here!" she said, looking about her. "What do you weed it for, when there's nobody to see?"

"Ah," said Mr Moggs, "you learn it doesn't do to let things go, in a garden, or anywhere else. Weeds and all such like, they get to thinking they own the place if you let 'em alone awhile."

He went on scratching out weeds, so Milly-Molly-Mandy gathered them into his big wheelbarrow for him.

Presently Mr Moggs scratched out a worm along with a tuft of dandelion, and Milly-Molly-Mandy squeaked because she nearly took hold of it without noticing (only she just didn't).

"Don't you like worms?" asked Mr Moggs.

"No," said Milly-Molly-Mandy, "I don't!"

"Ah," said Mr Moggs. "I know someone who does, though."

"Who?" asked Milly-Molly-Mandy, sitting back on her heels.

"Old Dum-dum's very partial to a nice fat worm," said Mr Moggs. "Haven't you met old Dum-dum?"

"No," said Milly-Molly-Mandy. "Who's old Dum-dum?"

"You come and see," said Mr Moggs. "I've got to feed him before I go off home."

He trundled the barrow to the back garden and emptied it on the rubbish heap, and Milly-Molly-Mandy followed, carrying the worm on a trowel.

Mr Moggs got a little tin full of grain from the tool-shed, and pulled a lettuce from the vegetable bed, and then he went to the end of the garden, Milly-Molly-Mandy following.

There was a little square of grass fenced off with wire netting in which was a little wooden gate. And in the middle of the square of grass was a little round pond. And standing at the edge of the little round pond, looking very solemn, hunched up in his feathers, was Dum-dum.

"Oh!" said Milly-Molly-Mandy. "Dum-dum is a duck!"

"Well, he's a drake, really," said Mr Moggs. "See the little curly feathers on his tail? That shows he's a gentleman. Lady ducks don't have curls on their tails." He leaned over the netting and emptied the grain into a feeding-pan lying on the grass. "Come on, quack-quack!" said Mr Moggs. "Here's your supper."

Dum-dum looked round at him, and at Milly-Molly-Mandy. Then he waddled slowly over on his yellow webbed feet, and shuffled his beak in the pan for a moment. Then he waddled slowly back to his pond, dipped down and took a sip, and stood as before, looking very solemn, hunched up in his feathers, with a drop of water hanging from his flat yellow beak.

"He doesn't want any supper!" said Milly-Molly-Mandy. "Why doesn't he?"

"Feels lonely, that's what. Misses the folk up at the Big House. They used to come and talk to him sometimes and give him bits. He's the little girl Jessamine's pet."

"Poor Dum-dum!" said Milly-Molly-Mandy. "He does look miserable. Would you like a worm, Dum-dum?"

He came waddling over again, and stretched up his beak. And down went the worm, *snip-snap*.

"Doesn't he make a funny husky noise? Has he lost his quack?" asked Milly-Molly-Mandy.

"No," said Mr Moggs, "gentlemen ducks never talk so loud as lady ducks."

"*Huh! Huh! Huh!*" quacked Dum-dum, asking for more worms as loudly as he could.

So Milly-Molly-Mandy dug with the trowel and found another, a little one, and threw it over the netting.

"Do you suppose worms mind very much?" she asked, watching Dum-dum gobbling.

"Well, I don't suppose they think a great deal about it, one way or t'other," said Mr Moggs.

He dug over a bit of ground with his spade, and Milly-Molly-Mandy found eight more worms. So Dum-dum had quite a good supper after all.

Then Milly-Molly-Mandy leaned over the wire-netting and tried stroking the shiny green feathers on Dum-dum's head and neck. And though he edged away a bit at first, after a few tries he stood quite still, holding his head down while she stroked as if he rather liked it.

And then suddenly he turned and pushed his beak into Milly-Molly-Mandy's warm hand and left it there, so that she was holding his beak as if she were shaking hands with it! It startled her at first, it felt so funny and cold.

"Ah, he likes you," said Mr Moggs, wiping his spade with a bunch of grass. "He's a funny old bird; some he likes and some he doesn't. Well, we must be going."

"Mr Moggs," begged Milly-Molly-Mandy, still holding Dum-dum's beak gently in her hand, "don't you think I might come in sometimes to cheer him up, while his people are away? He's so lonely!"

"Well," said Mr Moggs, "I don't see why not – if you don't go bringing your little playmates running around in here too. Look, if I'm not about you can get in by the side gate there." And he showed her how to unfasten it and lock it up again. "But mind, I'm trusting you," said Mr Moggs.

So Milly-Molly-Mandy promised to be very careful indeed.

After that she went into the Big House garden every day after school, to cheer up poor Dum-dum. And he got so cheerful he would run to his fence to meet her, saying *"Huh! Huh! Huh!"* directly he 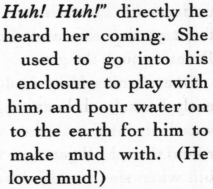 heard her coming. She used to go into his enclosure to play with him, and pour water on to the earth for him to make mud with. (He loved mud!)

One day Milly-Molly-Mandy thought it would be nice if Dum-dum could have a change from that narrow run, so she asked Mr Moggs if she might let him out for a little walk. And Mr Moggs said she might try it, if she watched that he didn't eat the flowers and vegetables or get out into the road. So Milly-Molly-Mandy opened his little wooden gate, and Dum-dum stepped out on his yellow feet, looking at everything with great interest.

He was so good and obedient, he followed her along the garden paths and came where she called, like a little dog. So she often let him out after that. She turned over stones and things for him to hunt slugs and woodlice underneath. Sometimes she took him in the front garden too, and showed him to Billy Blunt through the gate.

One morning Milly-Molly-Mandy was very early for school, because the clock at home was fast. At first, when she found no-one round the school gate, she thought it was late; but when she found it wasn't she knew why little-friend-Susan hadn't been ready when she passed the Moggs's cottage!

So, as there was plenty of time, she thought she'd go and visit Dum-dum before school today. So she slipped in by the side gate, and found him busily tidying his feathers in the morning sunshine. He looked surprised and very pleased to see her, and they had a run round the garden and found one slug and five woodlice (which Dum-dum thought very tasty for breakfast!). Then she shut him back in his enclosure, and latched his little gate, and shut the side gate and fastened it as Mr Moggs had shown her, and went off to school. (And she only just wasn't late, this time!)

Well, they'd sung the hymn, and Miss Edwards had called their names, and everybody was there except Billy Blunt and the new little girl called Bunchy. And they had just settled down for an arithmetic lesson when the little girl Bunchy hurried in, looking rather frightened. And she told Miss Edwards there was a great big goose outside, and she dared not come in before because she thought it might bite her!

"A goose!" said Miss Edwards. "Nonsense! There are no geese round here."

And Milly-Molly-Mandy looked up from her exercise book quickly. But she knew she had shut Dum-dum up carefully, so she went on again dividing by seven (which wasn't easy).

And then the door opened again, and Billy Blunt came in with a wide grin on his face and a note in his hand. (It was from his mother to ask Miss Edwards to excuse his being late, because he'd had to run an errand for his father, who had no-one else to send.)

And who *do* you think came in with him, pushing between Billy Blunt's legs through the doorway, right into the schoolroom?

It was Dum-dum!

"Billy Blunt!" said Miss Edwards. "What is this?"

"I couldn't help it, ma'am," said Billy Blunt. "He would come in. I tried to shoo him off." (But I don't really think he had tried awfully hard!)

"You mustn't let it come in here," said Miss Edwards. "Turn it out. Sit down, children, and be quiet." (Because they were all out of their places, watching and laughing at the duck that came to school.)

"Oh, please, Teacher," said Milly-Molly-Mandy, putting up her hand.

"Sit down, Milly-Molly-Mandy," said Miss Edwards. "Take that duck outside, Billy Blunt. Quickly, now."

But when Billy Blunt tried again to shoo him out Dum-dum slipped away from him, farther in, under the nearest desk. And Miss Muggins's Jilly squealed loudly, and pulled her legs up on to her seat.

"Please, Teacher –" said Milly-Molly-Mandy again. "Oh, please, Teacher – he's my duck. I mean, he's a friend of mine."

"What is all this?" said Miss Edwards. "Be quiet, all of you! Now, Milly-Molly-Mandy – explain."

So Milly-Molly-Mandy explained who Dum-dum was, and where he lived, and that she thought he had come to look for her – though how he had got out and found his way here she couldn't think. "Please, Teacher, can I take him back home?" she asked.

"I can't let you go in the middle of school," said Miss Edwards. "You can shut him out in the yard now, and take him back after school."

So Milly-Molly-Mandy walked to the door, saying, "Come, Dum-dum!"

And Dum-dum ran waddling on his flapping yellow feet after her, all across the floor, saying *"Huh! Huh! Huh!"* as he went.

How the children did laugh!

Billy Blunt said, "I'll just see that the gate's shut." And he hurried outside too (lest Miss Edwards should say he needn't!)

He tried to stroke Dum-dum as Milly-Molly-Mandy did, but Dum-dum didn't know Billy Blunt well enough. He opened his beak wide and said *"Huhhh!"* at him. So Billy Blunt left off trying and went and shut the gate.

"He must have some water," said Milly-Molly-Mandy (because she knew ducks are never happy if they haven't).

50

So they looked about for something to hold water, other than the drinking-mug. And Billy Blunt brought the lid of the dustbox, and they filled it at the drinking-tap and set it on the ground. And Dum-dum at once began taking sip after sip, as if he had never tasted such nice water before.

So Milly-Molly-Mandy and Billy Blunt left him there, and hurried back to their lessons.

Directly school was over the children rushed out to see Milly-Molly-Mandy lead the duck (drake, I mean) along the road back to his home. (It wasn't easy with so many people helping!) Mr Moggs was just coming away from the Big House, but he went back with

51

her to find out how Dum-dum had escaped,
for his gate was shut as Milly-Molly-Mandy
had left it. And they found Dum-dum had
made a little hole in his wire netting and
pushed through that way and under the front
gate. So Mr Moggs fastened up the hole.

And while he was doing it Milly-Molly-
Mandy noticed that the windows were open
in the Big House, and the curtains were
drawn back.

"Oh!" said Milly-Molly-Mandy. "Have the
people come back?"

"They're coming tomorrow," said Mr Moggs.
"Mrs Moggs is just airing the place for them."

"Then I shan't be able to come and see
Dum-dum any more!" said Milly-Molly-
Mandy.

And she felt quite sad for some days after
that, to think that Dum-dum wouldn't want
her any more, though she was glad he wasn't
lonely.

Then one day (what DO you think?) Milly-
Molly-Mandy met the little girl Jessamine and
her mother in the post-office, and the little girl
Jessamine's mother said, "Mr Moggs tells me

you used to come and cheer up our old duck while we were away!"

Milly-Molly-Mandy wondered if Mrs Green was cross about it. But she wasn't a bit. She said, "Jessamine is going to boarding school soon – did you know? – and she was wondering what to do about Dum-dum. Would you like to have him for keeps, when she has gone?"

And the little girl Jessamine said, "We want him to go to someone who'll be kind to him."

Milly-Molly-Mandy *was* pleased!

She ran home to give Father the stamps she had been sent to buy, and to ask the family if she might have Dum-dum for keeps.

And Mother said, "How kind of the Greens!"

And Father said, "He can live out in the meadow."

And Grandma said, "It will be very lonely for him."

And Grandpa said, "We must find him a companion."

And Aunty said, "You'll have to save up and buy another one."

And Uncle said, "I've been thinking of keeping a few ducks myself, down by the brook.
Your Dum-dum can live along with them, if
you like, Milly-Molly-Mandy."

Milly-Molly-Mandy was very pleased
indeed.

The next day she hurried down to the Big
House to tell the little girl Jessamine and her
mother. And they let her take Dum-dum home
with her at once.

So she led him slowly by the short cut
across the fields to the nice white cottage with
the thatched roof. And he followed her beautifully all the way. In fact, he walked right over
the step and into the kitchen with her!

When Uncle saw him following her about
he said:

"Milly-Molly had a duck.
    Its little head was green.
And everywhere that Milly went
    That duck was to be seen!"

"Yes, and he did follow me to school one
day, like Mary's little lamb!" said Milly-Molly-
Mandy.

And do you know, old Dum-dum didn't want to live down by the brook with the other ducks; it was too far from Milly-Molly-Mandy. He chose to live in the barn-yard with the cows and Twinkletoes the pony, and drink out of Toby the dog's drinking-bowl. And whenever the garden gate was undone Dum-dum would waddle straight through and make for the back door and knock on it with his beak, till Milly-Molly-Mandy came out to play with him!

5

MILLY-MOLLY-MANDY
AND THE GANG

ONCE UPON A TIME Milly-Molly-Mandy
was in Mr Smale the grocer's shop to get some
things for Mother. There was someone else
just being served, so while she waited she
looked from the doorway at Billy Blunt, who
was spinning a wooden top on the pavement
opposite, outside his father's corn-shop.

Presently some boys came along the road.
As they passed Billy Blunt one of the boys
kicked his top into the gutter, and another
pulled his cap off and threw it on the ground;
and then they went on down the road, laughing and shouting to one another.

Billy Blunt looked annoyed. But he only
picked up his cap and dusted it and put it on
again, and picked up his top and wiped it and
went on spinning.

And just then Mr Smale the grocer said, "Well, young lady, and what can I do for you this morning?" So Milly-Molly-Mandy had to come away from the door and be served.

Milly-Molly-Mandy had seen the boys before. They didn't belong to the village, but had come to stay near by, and they were always about, and always seemed to be making a lot of noise.

Well, Milly-Molly-Mandy got the things Mother wanted — a tin of cocoa, and a tin of mustard, and some root-ginger (for making rhubarb-and-ginger jam). And then she left the shop, to go across and speak to Billy Blunt.

But as she stepped over the step the boys were coming back again, up her side of the road this time, and they bumped into her so that the basket of groceries was knocked out of her hand. The tins came clattering out, and the paper of root-ginger burst all over the pavement.

And instead of saying "Sorry!" the boys only grinned broadly and went on their way, turning back to look at her now and then.

Billy Blunt came across the road to help.

"Billy!" said Milly-Molly-Mandy, "I believe they meant to do that! They bumped into me on purpose!"

Billy Blunt said, "Lot of donkeys." And began picking up bits of ginger.

"What did they want to do it for?" said Milly-Molly-Mandy. "And pull your cap off too!"

Billy Blunt only grunted, and picked up more bits of ginger.

Mr Smale the grocer came to his door to see what was going on, and said, "Them stupid young things knocked your basket, did they? Tell your mother to give that ginger a rinse in cold water and it'll be all right. Out to make nuisances of themselves, they are. They've got something to learn, stupid young things!"

Miss Muggins's niece, Jilly, came running

over. She had been watching from Miss Muggins's draper's shop opposite.

"They're a gang, they are," she told Milly-Molly-Mandy and Billy Blunt. "They try to knock people's hats off and make them drop things all the time. They've got a leader, and they're a gang!"

"They're donkeys," said Billy Blunt. And he went back to his own side of the pavement, winding up his top as he went.

Milly-Molly-Mandy said, "Thank you!" to him, and started off home with her basket. And Miss Muggins's Jilly went with her a little way, talking about "the gang" and the naughty things they did.

"They're silly," said Milly-Molly-Mandy. "I shouldn't take any notice of them."

"Oh, I don't," said Miss Muggins's Jilly. And she went right on talking about them till they came to the duck-pond. There they parted, and Milly-Molly-Mandy went on up the road to the nice white cottage with the thatched roof, where Mother was waiting for her groceries. (She washed the ginger, and it was quite all right.)

The next morning little-friend-Susan came round to see if Milly-Molly-Mandy was coming out to play.

Milly-Molly-Mandy was just helping Mother to clean the big preserving-pan that the rhubarb-and-ginger jam had been cooked in.

So Mother gave little-friend-Susan a spoon so that she could help to clean it too! And when the pan was as clean as they could make it with their two spoons they washed their sticky hands and faces, and then Mother gave them a big slice of bread-and-jam each to take out into the fields to eat.

So they went over the road and climbed the stile and strolled along the field-path, eating and talking and enjoying themselves very much.

And they were just turning down the lane leading to the Forge (which is always a nice way to go if you're not going anywhere special) when little-friend-Susan said, "Look at those boys; what are they doing?"

Milly-Molly-Mandy looked, licking jam off her fingers, and she saw they were the boys whom Miss Muggins's Jilly called "the gang". They were peeping round the hedge by the next stile.

"They're waiting to knock our hats off, only we haven't got any on!" said Milly-Molly-Mandy.

"Hadn't we better go back?" said little-friend-Susan.

"No!" said Milly-Molly-Mandy. "They're just silly, that's what they are. I'm going on."

So they went on, and climbed over the stile, Milly-Molly-Mandy first, and then little-friend-Susan.

And just as she had got over one of the boys jumped out of the hedge and knocked the piece of bread-and-jam (only a very small piece now) out of little-friend-Susan's hand into the dirt, and ran behind the hedge again.

Little-friend-Susan didn't like having her last piece of bread-and-jam spoiled. But Milly-Molly-Mandy even more didn't like seeing who the boy was who did it.

"It's Timmy Biggs," she said. "You know, that boy who won the race at the Fête, and Billy Blunt used to practise with. Why did he want to do that?"

Little-friend-Susan was looking at her bread-and-jam. "I can't eat this now," she said. "I'll take it to the ducks." (Because, of course, you never waste bread.)

So Milly-Molly-Mandy just called out, "You're silly, Timmy Biggs!" at the hedge, and they went on past the Forge and down to the duck-pond. (The blacksmith wasn't hammering or doing anything interesting, so they didn't stop to watch.)

Billy Blunt was in his garden by the corn-shop, busy with the lock of the old cycle-shed which stood in one corner. He saw them coming down the back lane, and as they didn't pass the garden fence he knew they must have turned

the other way. So presently he wandered out and found them by the duck-pond.

There were five ducks quacking and paddling in the water, and little-friend-Susan was tearing her bread into as many tiny bits as she could, but it didn't go very far!

"Hullo, Billy," said Milly-Molly-Mandy, as soon as he came near. "What do you think – Timmy Biggs has gone and joined that gang.

He knocked Susan's bread-and-jam into the dirt."

"I saw him with them," said Billy Blunt.

"We ought to do something," said Milly-Molly-Mandy.

"Umm," said Billy Blunt.

"Knock their caps off and see how they like it!" said little-friend-Susan.

"I don't see why we have to be silly just because they are," said Milly-Molly-Mandy. "I don't want to be in their sort of gang."

"Might start a gang of our own," said Billy Blunt.

"Oh, *yes*!" said Milly-Molly-Mandy and little-friend-Susan exactly together. (So then they had to hold each other's little finger and think of a poet's name before they did anything else. "Robert Burns!" said Milly-Molly-Mandy. "Shakespeare!" said little-friend-Susan.)

Then they set to work to think what they could do in their gang.

"It must be quite different from that other one," said Milly-Molly-Mandy. "They knock things down, so we pick things up."

"And they leave field-gates open, so we close them," said little-friend-Susan.

"And we could have private meetings in our old cycle-shed," said Billy Blunt. "It's got a lock and key."

That was a splendid idea, and the new gang got busy right away, clearing dust and spiders out of the cycle-shed. (There were no bicycles kept there now.)

And while they were in the middle of it – sweeping the floor with the garden broom, scraping the corners out with the garden trowel, and rubbing the tiny window with handfuls of grass – suddenly they heard shouting and footsteps running. And through the fence they saw boys tearing down the road from Mrs Jakes the postman's wife's gate.

"Come on," said Billy Blunt to his gang.

And they all ran out to see what had happened.

Mrs Jakes was in her yard, flapping her hands with annoyance, her clean washing lying all along the ground.

"Oh-h-h," she cried, "those boys! They untied the end of my clothes-line. And now look at it."

Billy Blunt picked up the end of the rope, and they all tried to lift the clothes-line to tie it up again, but it was too heavy with all the washing on it. So Mrs Jakes told them to un-peg the clothes and take them carefully off the ground, so as not to dirty them any more. The grass was clean and the things were nearly dry, so they weren't much hurt – only one or two tea-cloths needed to be rinsed where they had touched against the fence.

The new gang collected the pegs into a bas-ket, and helped Mrs Jakes to carry the wash-ing into her kitchen, and she was very grateful for their help.

"It's not near so bad as I thought when I first saw that line come down," she said. "Do you three like gooseberries?"

She gave them a handful each, and they went back to the cycle-shed and held a private meeting at once.

The next day Miss Muggins's Jilly found out about the new gang, and asked if she could join. She wanted to so much that they let her. And they made up some rules, such as not telling secrets of their private meetings, or where the key of the cycle-shed was hidden, and about being always on the look-out to pick things up, and mend things, and shut gates, and about being faithful to the rules of the gang, and that sort of thing.

Well, they were kept quite busy in one way and another. They helped Mrs Critch the thatcher's wife to collect her chickens when they were all let loose into the road. And they kept an eye on the field-gates, that cows and sheep didn't get a chance of straying. And they rescued hats and caps and things belonging to other children when they were knocked off unexpectedly. And whenever there was anything important to discuss or if any of their gang had anything given to them, such as apples, they would go along to the cycle-shed and call a private meeting.

They liked those meetings!

One day, when they had been having a meeting, they saw Timmy Biggs hanging about by the Blunts's fence, alone. And when Billy Blunt purposely wandered over that way Timmy Biggs said to him, "I say – I suppose you wouldn't let me join your gang? I don't

like that other one – I'd rather join yours.
Could I?"

Billy Blunt told him he'd have to think
about it and ask the others.

So he did, and they agreed to let Timmy
Biggs join, if he promised to keep the rules. So
he joined, and they started a rounders team on
the waste ground near the school.

Then two of the other boys took to hanging
round watching, as if they wanted to join in.
And presently they spoke to Billy Blunt.

"We don't like our gang much; we're tired of
it," they said. "It was his idea." And they
pointed at the third boy, who was sauntering
by himself down the lane. He had been their
gang leader.

With seven of them now they could play rounders splendidly, with Billy Blunt's bat, and Milly-Molly-Mandy and Miss Muggins's Jilly taking turns to lend their balls. The cycle-shed was too small now to hold their meetings, so they used it as a place to put the gang belongings in or to write important notices.

Not long after, just as the whole gang was going to begin a game, Milly-Molly-Mandy and Billy Blunt and little-friend-Susan began whispering together, and glancing at where the once-leader of the other gang was sitting under a tree, watching them (but pretending not to), because he had nothing much else to do.

When they had finished whispering Billy Blunt walked over to the tree.

"If you want to join in, come on," he said.

"Well, I don't mind," said the boy. And he got up quite quickly.

They had a grand game with so many players, and they worked up a very fine team indeed.

And do you know, when, a few weeks later, the time came for those three visiting boys to leave the village and go back home, nobody felt so very pleased to see them go.

And Milly-Molly-Mandy and Billy Blunt and little-friend-Susan and Miss Muggins's Jilly and Timmy Biggs would have been quite sorry, only that now they could just manage to squeeze into the cycle-shed to have their private meetings again!

6

MILLY-MOLLY-MANDY
FINDS A NEST

ONCE UPON A TIME, one warm summer morning, Uncle came quickly in at the back door of the nice white cottage with the thatched roof and shouted from the kitchen, "Milly-Molly-Mandy!"

Milly-Molly-Mandy, who was just coming downstairs carrying a big bundle of washing for Mother, called back, "Yes, Uncle?"

"Hi! quick!" said Uncle, and went outside the back door again.

Milly-Molly-Mandy couldn't think what Uncle wanted with her, but it had such an exciting sound she dropped the big bundle on the stairs in a hurry and ran down to the passage. But when she got to the passage she thought she ought not to leave the big bundle on the stairs, lest someone trip over it in the shadow; so she ran back again in a hurry and fetched the big bundle down, and ran along to the kitchen with it. But she was in such a hurry she dropped some things out of the big bundle and had to run back again and pick them up.

But at last she got them all on to the kitchen table, and then she ran out of the back door and said, "Yes, Uncle? What is it, Uncle?"

Uncle was just going through the meadow gate, with some boards under one arm and the tool-box on the other. He beckoned to Milly-Molly-Mandy with his head (which was the only thing he had loose to do it with), so Milly-Molly-Mandy ran after him down the garden path to the meadow.

"Yes, Uncle?" said Milly-Molly-Mandy.

"Milly-Molly-Mandy," said Uncle, striding over the grass with his boards and tool-box, "I've found a nest."

"What sort of a nest?" said Milly-Molly-

Mandy, hoppity-skipping a bit to keep up
with him.

"Milly-Molly-Mandy," said Uncle, "I rather
think it's a Milly-Molly-Mandy nest."

Milly-Molly-Mandy stopped and stared at
Uncle, but he strode on with his boards and
tool-box as if nothing had happened.

Then Milly-Molly-Mandy began jumping
up and down in a great hurry and said,
"What's a Milly-Molly-Mandy nest, Uncle?
What's it like, Uncle? Where is it, Uncle?
DO-O tell me!"

"Well," said Uncle, "you ought to know
what a Milly-Molly-Mandy nest is, being a
Milly-Molly-Mandy yourself. It's up in the big
old oak-tree at the bottom of the meadow."

So Milly-Molly-Mandy tore off to the big
old oak-tree at the bottom of the meadow, but
she couldn't see any sort of a nest there, only
Uncle's ladder leaning against the tree.

Uncle put the boards and tool-box carefully
down on the ground, then he settled the ladder
against the big old oak-tree, then he picked up
Milly-Molly-Mandy and carried her up the
ladder and sat her on a nice safe branch.

And then Milly-Molly-Mandy saw there was a big hollow in the big old oak-tree (which was a very big old oak-tree indeed). And it was such a big hollow that Uncle could get right inside it himself and leave quite a lot of room over.

"Now, Milly-Molly-Mandy," said Uncle, "you can perch on that branch and chirp a bit while I put your nest in order."

Then Uncle went down the ladder and brought up some of the boards and the tool-box, which he hung by its handle on a sticking-out branch. And Milly-Molly-Mandy watched while Uncle measured off boards and sawed them and fitted them and hammered nails into them, until he had made a beautiful flat floor in the hollow in the big old oak-tree, so that it looked like the nicest little fairy-tale room you ever saw!

Then he hoisted Milly-Molly-Mandy off the branch, where she had been chirping with excitement like the biggest sparrow you ever saw (only that you never saw a sparrow in a pink-and-white striped cotton frock), and heaved her up into the hollow.

And Milly-Molly-Mandy stood on the beautiful flat floor and touched the funny brown walls of the big old oak-tree's inside, and looked out of the opening on to the grass down below, and thought a Milly-Molly-Mandy nest was the very nicest and excitingest place to be in the whole wide world!

Just then whom should she see wandering along the road at the end of the meadow but little-friend-Susan!

"Susan!" called Milly-Molly-Mandy as loud as ever she could, waving her arms as hard as ever she could. And little-friend-Susan peeped over the hedge.

At first she didn't see Milly-Molly-Mandy up in her nest, and then she did, and she jumped up and down and waved; and Milly-Molly-Mandy beckoned, and little-friend-Susan ran to the meadow-gate and couldn't get it open because she was in such a hurry, and tried to get through and couldn't because she was too big, and began to climb over and couldn't because it was rather high. So at last she squeezed round the side of the gate-post through a little gap in the hedge and came

racing across the meadow to the big old oak-tree, and Uncle helped her up.

And then Milly-Molly-Mandy and little-friend-Susan sat and hugged themselves together, up in the Milly-Molly-Mandy nest.

Just then Father came by the big old oak-tree, and when he saw what was going on he went and got a rope and threw up one end to Milly-Molly-Mandy. And then Father tied an empty wooden box to the other end, and Milly-Molly-Mandy pulled it up and untied it and set it in the middle of the floor like a little table.

Then Mother, who had been watching from the gate of the nice white cottage with the thatched roof, came and tied an old rug to the end of the rope, and little-friend-Susan pulled it up and spread it on the floor like a carpet.

Then Grandpa came along, and he tied some fine ripe plums in a basket to the end of the rope, and Milly-Molly-Mandy pulled them up and set them on the little table.

Then Grandma came across the meadow bringing some old cushions, and she tied them to the end of the rope, and little-friend-Susan pulled them up and arranged them on the carpet.

Then Aunty came along, and she tied a little flower vase on the end of a rope, and Milly-Molly-Mandy pulled it up and set it in the middle of the table. And now the Milly-Molly-Mandy nest was properly furnished, and Milly-Molly-Mandy was in such a hurry to get Billy Blunt to come to see it that she could hardly get down from it quickly enough.

Mother said, "You may ask little-friend-Susan and Billy Blunt to tea up there if you like, Milly-Molly-Mandy."

So Milly-Molly-Mandy and little-friend-Susan ran off straight away, hoppity-skip to the Moggs's cottage (for little-friend-Susan to ask Mrs Moggs's permission), and to the village to Mr Blunt's corn-shop (to ask Billy

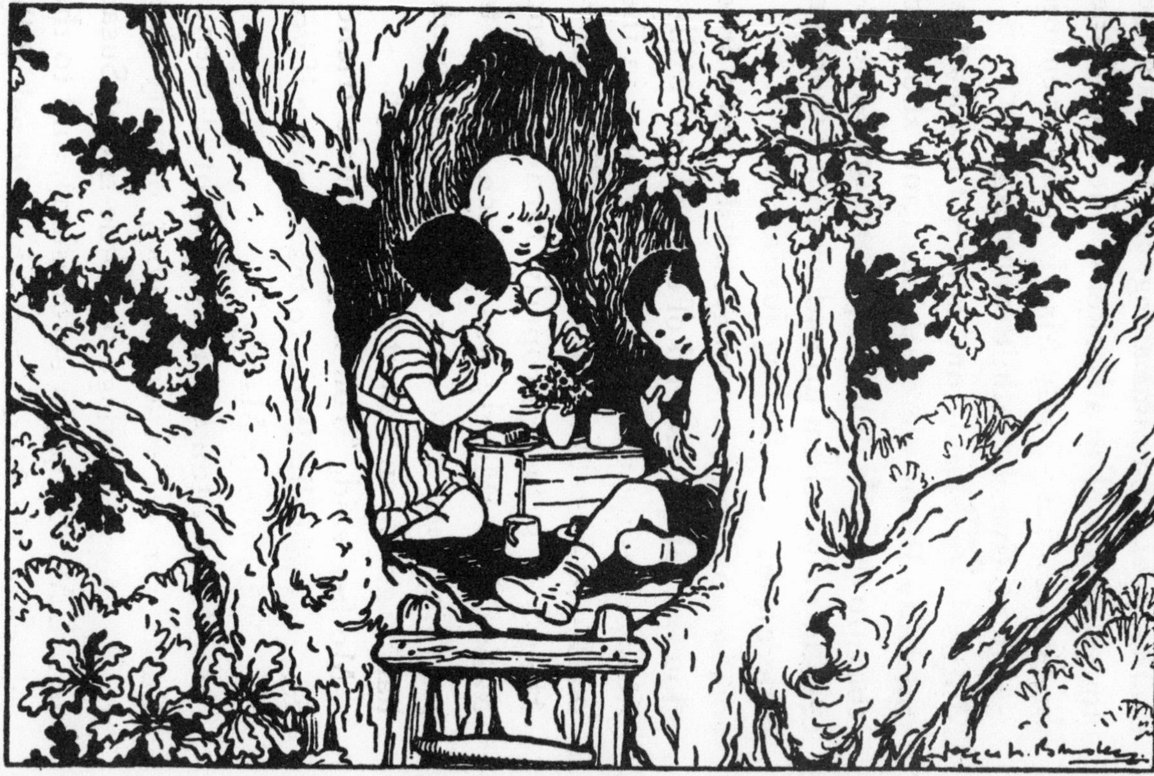

Up in the Milly-Molly-Mandy nest

Blunt), while Uncle fixed steps up the big old oak-tree, so that they could climb easily to the nest.

And at five o'clock that very afternoon Milly-Molly-Mandy and little-friend-Susan and Billy Blunt were sitting drinking milk from three little mugs and eating slices of bread-and-jam and gingerbread from three little plates, and feeling just as excited and comfortable and happy as ever they could be, up in the Milly-Molly-Mandy nest!

7

MILLY-MOLLY-MANDY
GOES FOR A PICNIC

ONCE UPON A TIME Milly-Molly-Mandy
was going for a picnic.

It was a real, proper picnic. Father and
Mother and Uncle and Aunty were all going
too, and little-friend-Susan and Billy Blunt
(because it wouldn't seem quite a real, proper
picnic without little-friend-Susan and Billy
Blunt).

They were going to take the red bus from
the crossroads to a specially nice picnic place,
where Milly-Molly-Mandy hadn't ever been
before because it was quite a long way off.
(The nicest places often do seem to be quite a
long way off, somehow.)

Grandpa and Grandma weren't going. They
said they would rather stay at home in the nice

white cottage with the thatched roof, and keep house and milk the cows if the picnickers weren't back in time.

It was a quiet, misty sort of morning, which looked as if it meant to turn out a fine hot day, as Father and Mother and Uncle and Aunty and Milly-Molly-Mandy (and Toby the dog) set off down the road to the village, carrying the picnic things.

When they came to the Moggs's cottage little-friend-Susan (in a clean cotton frock) was ready and waiting for them at the gate.

And when they came to Mr Blunt's corn-shop Billy Blunt (in a new khaki shirt with pockets) was ready and waiting for them by the side-door.

And when they came to the crossroads the red bus was already at the bus-stop. And as, of course, it wouldn't wait long for them, they all had to run like anything. But they just caught it, and climbed inside.

Father took the tickets.

Let's see: Father and Mother and Uncle and Aunty – that's four grown-up tickets. And little-friend-Susan and Billy Blunt and Milly-

Molly-Mandy — that's three half-tickets. (Father had asked the bus-conductor as they got on, "Do you mind the dog?" And the bus-conductor didn't, so Toby rode under the seat for nothing.)

Milly-Molly-Mandy said to little-friend-Susan and Billy Blunt as the bus went rattling along: "You haven't been to this place before, have you?" (hoping they hadn't).

Billy Blunt said: "Once. But I don't remember it. I was young then."

Little-friend-Susan said: "No. But my father and mother went a long time ago, and they say it's a nice place, and there's a wishing-well there, and you can drop a pin in and wish."

Billy Blunt said: "Don't believe in wishing-wells. Can't make things come true. Not if they aren't really."

And Milly-Molly-Mandy said: "Oh, neither do I. But it's fun to pretend!"

And little-friend-Susan thought so too.

When they came to the next village (where the bus turned round ready to go back again) they all had to get out and walk. Father and Mother and Uncle and Aunty walked in twos, and Milly-Molly-Mandy and little-friend-Susan and Billy Blunt walked all in a bunch. And Toby the dog ran here and there, snorting into holes and getting his nose muddy. (He did enjoy it!)

The sun shone hot now, and they began to get quite thirsty. But Mother said: "We're nearly there, and then you can have a nice drink at the well!" And Aunty gave them some fruit-sweets wrapped in coloured papers.

Milly-Molly-Mandy and little-friend-Susan

put their sweet-wrappers into their baskets, and Billy Blunt put his into one of his shirt pockets, to throw away when they got home.

Father said: "Well, anyone can see you've been properly brought up!"

He wished everyone who used that path did the same. He kept poking other people's bits of sweet-paper and orange-peel into the hedge with his stick as he went along, because they made the path look so nasty.

Mother said: "I think a place ought to look nicer because we've been there, not nastier!"

And Milly-Molly-Mandy and little-friend-Susan thought the same. Billy Blunt found a stick, and helped to poke the litter away too.

At last they came to the specially nice picnic place. And it really was almost like a fairy glen, with daisies and buttercups, and grassy slopes, and trees to climb, and a little stream running through the middle.

But – other people must have been there for picnics too, for – would you believe it? – they had left paper bags and egg-shells and litter everywhere. (And it almost spoiled every-where, I can tell you.)

"Oh dear!" said Father and Mother and Uncle and Aunty, looking all about.

"Where's the wishing-well?" asked Milly-Molly-Mandy and little-friend-Susan and Billy Blunt, looking all about too.

Father led the way to where some big, old trees were stooping round as if trying to hide something. And in behind them Milly-Molly-Mandy and little-friend-Susan and Billy Blunt saw a deep round hole in a wet rock which was simply covered over with beautiful green ferns and moss. And water, sparkling like crystal and cold as ice, was dripping down into it over the mossy rocks at the back.

It really did look just like a wishing-well!

Milly-Molly-Mandy and little-friend-Susan and Billy Blunt leaned over to see if they could see any pins lying at the bottom.

But – other people must have been there too, and – would you believe it? – they had thrown in old tins and ice-cream cartons and litter, and there it was all lying under the water that was clear as crystal and cold as ice.

"Oh, *dear*!" said Milly-Molly-Mandy and

little-friend-Susan and Billy Blunt. "Oh, dear, oh, dear!"

For you couldn't think of dropping a pin in and wishing there. You couldn't even have a drink.

Then Father said: "Mates, there's a spot of work to be done around here. We'd better get busy."

And he fished up some rusty tins out of the well with his stick.

Then Billy Blunt fished out some wet papers and cartons with his stick. And Milly-Molly-Mandy and little-friend-Susan picked up bits

of silver-paper and bus-tickets scattered about. And Father buried it all down a hole under a rock, where it couldn't be seen.

The well didn't look clear now, but Father said it would soon settle and be crystal clear again, as a wishing-well should be. So they thought they had better wait before making their wishes.

Meantime Mother and Aunty had chosen the best spot for the picnic, so Milly-Molly-Mandy and little-friend-Susan and Billy Blunt got busy collecting all the scraps of paper lying about, and Uncle put a match to them. (He took good care to do it where nothing else could catch fire or hurt the growing things, because, of course, when you have roots like trees and plants you can't move out of the way when you're getting hurt!) Billy Blunt collected bits of broken glass too, lest Toby the dog should cut his paws, and Father buried it safely.

By then it was time for the picnic, so they all washed their hands in the little stream running through the middle, and sat down to enjoy themselves.

They had hard-boiled eggs, and brown bread-and-butter, and cheese, and tomatoes, and buns and a big jam-tart. And to drink there was hot tea from a Thermos for the grown-ups, and cold milk for the young ones. And they were all so thirsty they drank up every drop. (Toby the dog drank all he wanted from the little stream.)

When everyone had quite done they packed everything tidily away in their baskets to take home with them, all their empty bottles and wrapping-papers and string.

And then Father gave a great sigh of satisfaction, and lay back in the sunshine and put his hat over his face. And Mother sat in the shade and took up her knitting. And Uncle pulled out his newspaper with the crossword puzzle. And Aunty opened her nice new lady's magazine.

But Milly-Molly-Mandy and little-friend-Susan and Billy Blunt (and Toby the dog) all wanted to be up and doing. So they ran about, paddling in the little stream and climbing the trees and playing hide-and-seek. And wherever they went they tidied up until there wasn't a bit of litter to be seen.

"Well!" said Milly-Molly-Mandy, looking about when it was almost time to go. "This picnic place looks ever so much nicer now *we've* visited it! I should think the next people would be pleased."

"I wish," said little-friend-Susan, "everybody would leave nice places nice when they visit them."

That made Billy Blunt remember something. And he said:

"We never made our wishes at the wishing-well."

So they all three rushed over to the wishing-well. And there it was, clear as crystal and cold as ice right down to the bottom, as a wishing-well should be. Mother gave them a cup, and they all drank, and filled up their bottle.

"Dropping just a pin in won't spoil it now, will it?" said Milly-Molly-Mandy.

"We can't make a proper wish without a pin," said little-friend-Susan.

"Won't make any difference anyhow," said Billy Blunt.

But he looked a bit disappointed, all the same, when Mother could find only two pins, which she gave to Milly-Molly-Mandy and little-friend-Susan. But then Father found one under his coat lapel, and handed it to Billy Blunt. And Billy Blunt looked quite pleased as he took it!

So they each dropped a pin into the wishing-well, and solemnly wished.

They couldn't tell their wishes out loud, because that might have spoiled the magic! But I *think* they all wished the same wish. And as Father said, if enough people wish a wish, and it's a *good* wish, it's quite likely to come to pass.

So let's hope that Milly-Molly-Mandy's and little-friend-Susan's and Billy Blunt's wishes all come true!

8

MILLY-MOLLY-MANDY
HAS A CLEAN FROCK

ONCE UPON A TIME, one beautiful, fine morning, Milly-Molly-Mandy came out in a nice clean frock. (Not for any special reason; only, of course, you have to have a clean frock sometimes, and a beautiful, fine morning seems a good enough reason.)

It was a Monday morning, so Mother was busy with the washing. Milly-Molly-Mandy helped her to get out the tin baths, and put up the washing-lines in the garden, and find the clothes-pegs. For with Father and Grandpa and Grandma and Uncle and Aunty and Milly-Molly-Mandy and herself to wash for, Mother always had quite a busy time on Monday mornings.

"Well, now I think that will do, thank you,

Milly-Molly-Mandy," said Mother at last. "You can run off and play now."

So Milly-Molly-Mandy called Toby the dog, and they went skipping off together in the beautiful sunshine, down the road with the hedges each side, to see if little-friend-Susan or Billy Blunt were coming out to play. She had only gone as far as the big meadow gate when whom did she see but Billy Blunt (in a nice clean shirt), coming walking along up from the village. So Milly-Molly-Mandy waved hard and called out:

"Hullo, Billy! Where are you going?"

Billy Blunt just came walking on till he got near enough (so that he needn't bother to shout), and then he held up an empty jam-jar he was carrying and said:

"Tadpoles."

"Oh!" said Milly-Molly-Mandy. "Where are you going to get them? What are you going to do with them? Can I come and help you?"

Billy Blunt said:

"I want to watch them turn into frogs in our water-butt."

Milly-Molly-Mandy said:

"There's tadpoles sometimes in the pond where the cows drink."

"I know," said Billy Blunt. "That's where I'm going. Come on."

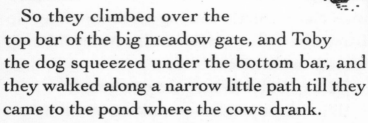

So they climbed over the top bar of the big meadow gate, and Toby the dog squeezed under the bottom bar, and they walked along a narrow little path till they came to the pond where the cows drank.

Toby the dog ran off at once to the steep part to look for water-rats. Billy Blunt and Milly-Molly-Mandy walked round to the shallow part to look for tadpoles. But the pond was getting very low, and it was very muddy and trampled there. They couldn't get close without mud coming right over their shoes.

After a while they heard Toby the dog barking excitedly, because he had found a rat-hole and wanted the owner to come out and be caught. (As if any sensible rat would!) But presently the barking turned to a splashing and yelping, so Milly-Molly-Mandy and Billy Blunt ran along the bank to see what had happened.

And – goodness me! – somehow or other Toby the dog must have slipped over the edge, for there he was, right in the pond. And he *was* in a mess! – all covered with mud and weedy stuff.

"He can't climb out there – it's too steep," said Billy Blunt. And he called, "Come on, Toby!" and tried to lead him along to where the bank was lower.

But Toby the dog just kept trying to scramble out where he had slipped in.

"He can't swim through that mud and weedy stuff, that's why," said Milly-Molly-Mandy. And she reached down to try to pull him out. But she just couldn't get him, so she reached over farther.

And then – goodness me! – somehow or other she must have reached over too far, for next moment there was Milly-Molly-Mandy in the pond too. And she *was* in a mess! – all covered with moss and weedy stuff.

Billy Blunt said: "Well! Of all the cuckoos!" And he reached down to try to pull her out.

Milly-Molly-Mandy said: "Let's get Toby out first."

So they got Toby the dog out on to the bank. And directly he found himself there Toby the dog shook himself violently, and mud and weedy stuff flew out all round, right over Billy Blunt's clean shirt.

Billy Blunt stepped back in a hurry.

And then – goodness me! – somehow or other he must have stepped over the edge of the bank, for next moment there was Billy Blunt in the pond now (nearly on top of

Milly-Molly-Mandy). And he *was* in a mess! – all covered with mud and weedy stuff.

(Milly-Molly-Mandy might have said: "Well! Of all the cuckoos!" But she was really too busy just then.)

The pond wasn't deep, and they were able to scramble out all right. But – goodness me! – you NEVER did see such a mess as Milly-Molly-Mandy and Billy Blunt and Toby the dog were in! – all covered with mud and weedy stuff.

"Oh, dear!" said Milly-Molly-Mandy. "Now what shall we do?"

"Umm," said Billy Blunt. "What will my mother say?"

"Will she be very cross?" asked Milly-Molly-Mandy. "You couldn't help it."

Billy Blunt only said: "It was a clean shirt." And he tried to squeeze the water out of it.

Milly-Molly-Mandy said: "My dress was clean too." And she tried to squeeze the water out of it.

But the more they squeezed the worse things seemed to get.

"We'd better go home," said Billy Blunt at last.

"Let's go to my home first," said Milly-Molly-Mandy. "P'raps Mother will know what to do before your mother sees you."

Billy Blunt said: "Well – I suppose I'd better see you get home all right, anyhow."

So they went across the fields and through two hedges, instead of by the road (so that nobody should see them). And they crept through the back gate into the garden of the nice white cottage with the thatched roof (where Milly-Molly-Mandy lived).

Mother was busy hanging sheets out on the line, and she didn't notice them at first.

So Milly-Molly-Mandy said: "Mother," (but not very loudly).

And Mother turned round. And she saw them standing there, Milly-Molly-Mandy, and Billy Blunt, and Toby the dog, all covered with mud and weedy stuff.

"OH!" said Mother

"We fell in the cow-pond," said Milly-Molly-Mandy in a small voice. "Toby fell in first and I tried to get him out and I fell in and Billy tried to get me out and he fell in and – we're very sorry, Mother."

And Billy Blunt nodded.

"Oh!" said Mother again.

And then she said: "Stay there!"

And she went indoors.

So Milly-Molly-Mandy and Billy Blunt and Toby the dog stayed there, wondering what Mother meant to do with them, and if she were very cross. Milly-Molly-Mandy wanted to wipe the mud off her face, but her hand was too dirty. Billy Blunt wanted to blow his nose, but his handkerchief was too wet. Toby the dog rolled in the dust to dry himself. (But it didn't make him look better.)

When Mother came out again she was carrying the tin bath she used for the washing, and after her came Aunty carrying the tin bath used for the rinsing, and they set them down on the grass. Then they went indoors and came out again, Mother with a big kettle and some soapflakes, Aunty with a big bucket and some towels. When they had put warm water in the two tin baths, Mother emptied the whole packet of soapflakes in and swished around with her hand in each till the bubbles rose up, and up, and UP.

Then Mother took Milly-Molly-Mandy, and Aunty took Billy Blunt, and they peeled the clothes off them and plopped them into the two tin baths then and there!

"Now!" said Mother. "Get busy and clean yourselves."

And she gathered up the dirty clothes into the bucket and pumped water over them at the pump.

So there were Milly-Molly-Mandy and Billy Blunt that beautiful fine morning, each in a bathful of warm bubbles nearly up to their necks, with the sheets flapping round them, and the sun shining, and the birds singing...

Then they got busy, swishing about in their baths, making more and yet more bubbles. They lathered their heads till they looked as if they had curly white hair and beards. They blew great coloured bubbles between their hands and watched them float off into the sky. They threw handfuls of bubbles at Toby the dog, which he tried to catch as the wind carried them away between the clothes that Mother and Aunty were pegging up on the clothes-lines.

Goodness me! Those were nice baths

Soon Milly-Molly-Mandy and Billy Blunt were really enjoying themselves like anything, laughing and shouting, with Toby the dog barking and the sun shining and the birds singing.

Goodness me! Those were nice baths!

And you can't think how *clean* they both felt when at last Mother made Milly-Molly-Mandy get out into a big towel and hurried her indoors to put something dry on, and Billy Blunt got out into another big towel and Mother lent him some pyjamas of Father's to put on.

Then Mother washed their clothes in one of the baths and Aunty caught Toby the dog and washed him in the other. And then they threw the water out and washed the baths!

Then Milly-Molly-Mandy came out in a dressing-gown (because both her dresses were in the wash), and she and Billy Blunt, in big pyjamas, sat in the sun together, drying their hair and eating biscuits while their clothes flapped on the line and Toby the dog rolled in dust to get the cleanness off him. (He was the only one who didn't enjoy his bath.)

Mother quickly ironed up Billy Blunt's shirt and shorts and Milly-Molly-Mandy's pink-and-white striped frock. And when they put them on again you would never dream what they had been up to that beautiful, fine morning.

"Well," said Milly-Molly-Mandy, "I am sorry we got so dirty, Mother, but I *did* like that bubble-bath!"

"Yes," said Billy Blunt. "I wouldn't care if I had to have a bubble-bath every day!"

But Mother said:

"Now listen, you two. Maybe you couldn't help it this time. But if you come home like

that *again* you won't have bubble-baths!
I shall put you in the cow-trough and turn
the pump on you! This has been the biggest
washing-day I've had, and I don't want
another like it."

So then Billy Blunt said: "No, ma'am. I'm
very much obliged to you, ma'am." And he
thanked Aunty too.

Then he went off home in his nice clean
things, sure that his mother would never
dream what he had been up to.

But when Mrs Blunt saw him come in
(rather late for dinner, but looking so clean
and tidy) she guessed he had been up to *something*. And when she saw his muddy shoes,
and found he hadn't caught any tadpoles and
didn't know what he had done with his jam-
jar, she pretty well guessed everything.

But Mrs Blunt never dreamed what grand
bubble-baths Billy Blunt and
Milly-Molly-Mandy had had, out in
the garden of the nice white cottage with the thatched roof that
beautiful fine morning!

9

MILLY-MOLLY-MANDY
DRESSES UP

ONCE UPON A TIME Milly-Molly-Mandy
found an old skirt. She and little-friend-Susan
were playing up in the attic of the nice white
cottage with the thatched roof (where Milly-
Molly-Mandy lived). They
had turned out the rag-bags
and dressed themselves in all
sorts of things – blouses with
the sleeves cut off, worn-out
curtains, old night-gowns
and shirts, and some of
Milly-Molly-Mandy's
own out-grown frocks
(which Mother kept for
patching her present
ones, when needed).

Milly-Molly-Mandy and little-friend-Susan looked awfully funny – especially when they tried to put on the things which Milly-Molly-Mandy had outgrown. They laughed and laughed.

(The attic was rather a nice place for laughing in – it sort of echoed.)

Well, when Milly-Molly-Mandy found the old skirt of Mother's, of course she put it on. The waist had to fasten round her chest to make it short enough, but that didn't matter. She put on over it an old jumper with a burnt place in front, but she wore it back to front; so that didn't matter either.

Milly-Molly-Mandy walked up and down the attic, feeling just like Mother. She even wore a little brass curtain-ring on the finger of her left hand like Mother.

And then she had an idea.

"Let's both dress up and be ladies," said Milly-Molly-Mandy.

"Ooh, yes, let's," said little-friend-Susan.

So they picked out things from the rag-bags as best they could, and little-friend-Susan put on a dress which was quite good in front, only it had no back. She pulled her curls up on to the top of her head and tied them there with a bit of ribbon.

Milly-Molly-Mandy tucked her hair behind her ears and fastened it behind with a bit of string, so that it made a funny sort of bun.

"We ought to wear coats and hats," said Milly-Molly-Mandy, "then we'd look quite all right."

So they went downstairs in their long skirts, and Milly-Molly-Mandy took Aunty's mackintosh from the pegs by the kitchen door for little-friend-Susan, and she borrowed an old jacket of Mother's for herself. They borrowed their hats too (not their best ones, of course), and went up to Mother's room to look in the mirror. They trimmed themselves up a bit from the rag-bags, and admired each other, and strutted about, enjoying themselves like anything.

And just then Mother called up the stairs:

"Milly-Molly-Mandy?"

"Yes, Mother?" Milly-Molly-Mandy called down the stairs.

"When you go out, Milly-Molly-Mandy, please go to the grocer's and get me a tin of treacle. I shall be wanting some for making gingerbread. I've put the money on the bottom stair here."

So Milly-Molly-Mandy said: "Yes, Mother. I'll just go, Mother."

And then Milly-Molly-Mandy looked at little-friend-Susan. And little-friend-Susan looked at Milly-Molly-Mandy. And they said to each other, both at the same time:

"DARE you to go and get it like this!"

"Ooh!" said Milly-Molly-Mandy; and "Ooh!" said little-friend-Susan. "*Dare* we?"

"I'd have to tuck up my sleeves — they're too long," said Milly-Molly-Mandy. "Tell you what, Susan, we might go by the fields instead of down the road; then we wouldn't meet so many people. Look, I'll carry a shopping-basket, and you can take an umbrella, because it's easier when you've got something to carry. Come on."

So Milly-Molly-Mandy and little-friend-Susan crept downstairs and out at the front door, so that Father and Mother and Grandpa and Grandma and Uncle and Aunty mightn't see them. And they went down the front path to the gate.

But there was a horse and cart clip-clopping along the road, so they hung back and waited till it went by. And what do you think? The man driving it saw someone's back-view behind the gate, and he must have taken for granted it was Mother or Aunty or Grandma, for he called out, "Morning, ma'am!" as he passed.

Milly-Molly-Mandy and little-friend-Susan were so pleased they laughed till they had to hold each other up. But it made them feel much better.

They straightened their hats and hitched their skirts, and then they opened the gate and walked boldly across the road to the stile in the hedge on the other side.

It was quite a business getting over that stile. Milly-Molly-Mandy and little-friend-Susan had to rearrange themselves carefully again on the other side.

Then, with their basket and umbrella, the two ladies set off along the narrow path across the field.

"Now, we mustn't laugh," said Milly-Molly-Mandy. "Ladies don't laugh a lot, not outdoors. We shall give ourselves away if we keep laughing."

"No," said little-friend-Susan, "we mustn't. But suppose we meet Billy Blunt?"

"We mustn't run, either," said Milly-Molly-Mandy. "Ladies don't run much."

"No," said little-friend-Susan, "we mustn't. But I do hope we don't meet Billy Blunt."

"So do I," said Milly-Molly-Mandy. "I'd like to meet him worst of anybody. He'd be sure to know us. We mustn't keep looking round, either, Susan. Ladies don't keep on looking round."

"I was only wondering if anyone could see us," said little-friend-Susan.

But there were only cows on the far side of the meadow, and they weren't at all interested in the two rather short ladies walking along the narrow path.

Soon Milly-Molly-Mandy and little-friend-Susan came to the stile into Church Lane. This was a rather high stile, and while she was getting over it the band of Milly-Molly-Mandy's skirt slipped from her chest to her waist, and her feet got tangled in the length of it. She came down on all fours into the grass at the side, with her hat over one eye. But, luckily, she just got straightened up before they saw the old gardener-man who looked after the churchyard coming along up the lane with his wheel-barrow.

"Let's wait till he's gone," said Milly-Molly-Mandy. "We'll be looking in my basket, so we needn't look up."

So they rummaged in the basket (which held only a bit of paper

114

with the money in it), and talked in ladylike tones, until the old gardener-man had passed by.

He stared rather, and looked back at them once, but the two ladies were too busy to notice him.

When he was safely through the churchyard gate they went down the lane till they came to the forge at the bottom. Mr Rudge the black-smith was banging away on his anvil. He was a nice man, and Milly-Molly-Mandy and little-friend-Susan thought it would be fun to stop and see what he thought of them. So they stood at the doorway and watched him hammering at a piece of red-hot iron he was holding with his tongs.

Mr Rudge glanced up at them. And then he looked down. And then he went on hammer-ing. And then he turned and put the piece of iron into the furnace. And while he worked the handle of the big bellows slowly up and down (to make the fire burn hot) he looked at them again over his shoulder, and said:

"Good morning, ladies. It's a warm day today."

"Yes, it is," agreed Milly-Molly-Mandy and little-friend-Susan. (They were feeling very warm indeed, though it wasn't at all sunny out.)

"Visitors in these parts, I take it," said the blacksmith.

"Yes, we are," agreed Milly-Molly-Mandy and little-friend-Susan.

Then Milly-Molly-Mandy said: "Can you tell us if there is a good grocer's shop any-where round here?"

"Let me see, now," said the blacksmith, thinking hard. "Yes, I believe there is. Try going to the end of this lane, here, and turn sharp right – very sharp, mind. Then look both ways at once, and cross the road. You'll maybe see one."

Then he took his iron out, all red-hot, and began hammering at it again to shape it.

Milly-Molly-Mandy and little-friend-Susan couldn't be quite sure whether Mr Rudge knew them or not. They were just thinking of going on when – WHO should come round the corner of Mr Blunt's corn-shop but Billy Blunt himself!

Billy Blunt noticed the two
rather odd-looking ladies
standing in front of the
forge. And he noticed one
of them pull the other's
sleeve, which came right
down over her hand. And
then they both turned and
walked up the lane.

He thought they looked
a bit queer somehow – short and rather
crumpled. So he stopped at the forge and
asked the blacksmith:

"Who are those two?"

"Lady-friends of mine," said the blacksmith, turning the iron and getting hold of
it in a different place. "Lady-friends. Known
'em for years."

Billy Blunt waited, but the blacksmith didn't
say anything more. So he began strolling up
the lane after the two ladies, who were near
the stile by now.

The lady in the mackintosh seemed to be a
bit flustered, whispering to the other. Then the
other one said (so that he could hear):

"I seem to have lost my shopping-list, it isn't in my basket. Have you got it, dear?"

Billy Blunt strolled nearer. He wanted to see their faces.

"No, I haven't got it," said the first one. "We'd better go home and look for it. Oh, dear, I think it's coming on to rain. I felt a little spit. I must put up my umbrella."

And she opened it and held it over them both, so that Billy Blunt couldn't see so much of them.

He strolled a bit nearer, and stopped to pick an unripe blackberry from the hedge and put it in his mouth. He wanted to see the ladies climb over the stile.

But they waited there, rummaging in their basket and talking of the rain. Billy Blunt couldn't feel any rain. Presently he heard the lady with the basket say in a rather pointed way:

"I wonder what that *little boy* thinks he's doing there? He ought to go home."

And, quite suddenly, that's what the "little boy" did. At any rate he hurried off down the lane and out of sight.

Then Milly-Molly-Mandy and little-friend-Susan, very relieved, picked up their skirts and scrambled over the stile, and set off back across the fields. There was nobody to see them now but the cows, so they ran, laughing and giggling and tumbling against each other among the buttercups all the way across.

And by the time they got back to the first stile, just opposite the nice white cottage with the thatched roof (where Milly-Molly-Mandy lived), you never saw such a funny-looking pair of ladies!

Little-friend-Susan's hat-trimming had come off, and Milly-Molly-Mandy had stepped right out of her rag-bag skirt after it had tripped her up three times, and they were both so out of breath with giggling that they could hardly climb over on to the road.

But the moment they landed on the other side somebody jumped out at them from the hedge. And WHO do you suppose it was?

Yes, of course! It was Billy Blunt.

He had run all the way round by the road, just for the fun of facing them as they came across that stile.

"Huh! Think I didn't know you?" he asked, breathing hard. "I knew you at once."

"Then why didn't you speak to us?" asked little-friend-Susan.

"Think I'd want to speak to either of you looking like that?" said Billy Blunt, grinning.

"I don't believe you did know us, not just at once," said Milly-Molly-Mandy, "or you'd have said something, even if it was rude!"

"Look!" said little-friend-Susan. "There's someone coming. Let's go in quick!"

So they scurried across the road and through the garden gate. And just then Milly-Molly-Mandy's mother came out to pick a handful of flowers for the table.

"Well, goodness me!" said Mother. "Whatever's all this?"

"We were just dressing up," said Milly-Molly-Mandy, "when you wanted us to go to the village."

"And we dared each other to go like this," said little-friend-Susan.

"I saw the two guys talking to the blacksmith," said Billy Blunt.

"Anyhow," said Milly-Molly-Mandy, hopping on each leg in turn, her rag-bag hat-trimming looping over one eye, "we did dare, didn't we, Susan?"

"Well, well!" said Mother. "And where's my tin of treacle?"

Milly-Molly-Mandy stopped.

"We forgot all about it! I'm sorry, Mother. We'll go now!"

"Not like that!" said Mother. "You take my coat off, and go in and tidy yourselves first. And the attic too."

"I'll run and get the treacle for you," said Billy Blunt. "'Spect I stopped 'em – they'd got almost as far as the grocer's, anyhow."

"Yes, he scared us!" said Milly-Molly-Mandy, handing him Mother's money out of the basket. "He followed us along and never said a word. He thought we were proper ladies, that's why!"

"Thought you were proper guys," said Billy Blunt, going out of the gate.

10

MILLY-MOLLY-MANDY
AND THE GOLDEN WEDDING

ONCE UPON A TIME Milly-Molly-Mandy
was busy dipping fingers of bread-and-butter
into her boiled egg at supper-time, and listening while Father and Mother and Grandpa
and Grandma and Uncle and Aunty talked.

They were counting how long it was that
Grandpa and Grandma had been married.
And it was a very long time indeed – nearly
fifty years!

Grandma said: "Our Golden Wedding –
next month!"

Milly-Molly-Mandy was
very interested, though she
did not know what a Golden
Wedding was. But it
sounded rather grand.

"Do you have to be

married all over again when you've been married fifty years?" she asked.

"No," said Mother; "its more like having a very special sort of birthday. When you've been married twenty-five years you have a Silver Wedding Day, and people give you silver presents. But when you've been married fifty years it's a Golden one. We shall have to think what we can do to celebrate Grandpa's and Grandma's Golden Wedding Day. Dear me!"

Milly-Molly-Mandy whispered: "Do we have to give golden presents to Grandpa and Grandma?"

Mother whispered back: "We shall have to think what we can do about it, Milly-Molly-Mandy. But there are different sorts of gold, you know – sunshine and buttercups and, well, little girls, even, can be good as gold sometimes! We shall have to think."

Grandpa (eating his kipper) heard their whisperings, and said: "If Milly-Molly-Mandy promises to be as good as gold that day you can just wrap her up in tissue-paper and hand her over. She'll do for a Golden Wedding present!"

123

But Milly-Molly-Mandy wouldn't promise to be as good as all that!

She did wonder, though, what sort of gold presents Father and Mother and Uncle and Aunty would be giving to Grandpa and Grandma. And she wondered too, very much, what sort of a gold present she herself could give. It was important to think of something very special for such a special occasion.

She talked with little-friend-Susan and Billy Blunt about it before school next morning.

Little-friend-Susan said: "I'd like to give a present too. But I haven't enough money."

Billy Blunt said: "I'd be rich if I could give anybody a gold present!"

"But it doesn't always have to be that sort of present," Milly-Molly-Mandy told them. "There's good-as-gold, if we could think of something like that. Only I can't think what."

And then they met others on their way in to school, and had other things to think about.

A few days later Billy Blunt showed Milly-Molly-Mandy a crumpled bit of newspaper he had in his pocket, and made her read it. It was something about a golden-jubilee concert somewhere. Milly-Molly-Mandy couldn't think why Billy Blunt bothered to keep it.

"Plain as your nose," said Billy Blunt. "Golden jubilee means fifty years, like your Golden Wedding business. They're having a concert to celebrate. Thought you might be interested."

And then, suddenly, Milly-Molly-Mandy was very interested.

"You mean *we* might do something like that for Grandpa and Grandma? Oh, Billy! what a good idea. What can we do?"

But Billy Blunt only said: "Oh, it was just an idea."

And he went off to exchange foreign stamps

with a friend of his, Timmy Biggs. So Milly-Molly-Mandy looked for little-friend-Susan to tell her.

"But what could we do for a concert?" asked little-friend-Susan. "We can't play or anything."

But Milly-Molly-Mandy said (like Mother): "We shall have to think, Susan!"

The Golden Wedding meant a lot of thinking for everybody – Father and Mother and Uncle and Aunty as well.

Mother had the first idea. She said (while Grandpa and Grandma were out of the way): "I shall make a big golden wedding-cake, iced with yellow icing, and trimmed with gold hearts and a gold paper frill. We'll have a Golden Wedding tea-party!"

Father and Uncle and Aunty and Milly-Molly-Mandy thought that was a grand idea!

After school next morning Milly-Molly-Mandy and little-friend-Susan and Billy Blunt looked in Miss Muggins's shop window to see if there was anything interesting there besides socks and dusters and underclothes.

"There's a little gold bell with a handle on that shelf – see," said Milly-Molly-Mandy, "and pins with gold heads."

"Those yellow pencils with gold tops look quite cheap," said little-friend-Susan, "and that Happy Returns card with gold print!"

(Really, there seemed quite a number of gold things if you kept your eyes open!)

Billy Blunt looked carefully, but said nothing.

"Have you thought what you can do at the concert?" Milly-Molly-Mandy asked him.

"What concert?" said Billy Blunt.

"Our Golden Wedding concert, of course!" said Milly-Molly-Mandy.

"Huh!" said Billy Blunt. And then he said: "Better call a meeting and make plans."

"Ooh, yes let's!" said Milly-Molly-Mandy and little-friend-Susan together. And Milly-Molly-Mandy added, "Somewhere secret, where Grandpa and Grandma won't know!"

Billy Blunt said they might come to his place after tea on Saturday; his folk would be in the corn-shop, and they could plan in private there.

So directly after tea on Saturday Milly-Molly-Mandy met little-friend-Susan at the Moggs's gate, and they ran together down to the village, and through the gate at the side of the corn-shop, and up the garden path into the Blunts's house.

"Oh, it's you," said Billy Blunt (as if he wasn't expecting them).

Milly-Molly-Mandy hadn't seen inside the Blunts's sitting-room before, only in the corn-shop. It was small and rather dark, but very cosy, with a thick red cloth on the table.

"Sit down," said Billy Blunt. "The meeting's begun. I'm President, as it's my house."

"But it's *my* Golden Wedding," Milly-Molly-Mandy told him.

They laughed at that (because Milly-Molly-Mandy didn't look over fifty), and then they felt more at home.

Billy Blunt thumped on the table, and said, "Order, now!"

And they settled down to thinking what they could do about a concert.

They couldn't play the piano, though there was one which Aunty played on at the nice white cottage with the thatched roof (where, of course, Milly-Molly-Mandy lived). Billy Blunt had an old mouth-organ, but it was broken. And little-friend-Susan had a dulcimer, but her baby sister played with it and half the notes were gone.

"Then we'll have to make up things," said Milly-Molly-Mandy. "I can play a comb and tissue-paper!"

"Saucepan lids make awfully nice clappers," said little-friend-Susan.

Billy Blunt reached down and picked up the shovel and poker from the fireplace and started hitting them together, till Milly-Molly-Mandy and little-friend-Susan shouted at him that Grandpa and Grandma wouldn't like that one bit! So then he put the shovel to his shoulder and sawed up and down it with the poker, singing, "Tweedle-tweedle-tweedle," exactly as if he were playing the violin!

129

Milly-Molly-Mandy and little-friend-Susan did wish they had thought of that first!

"Well!" said Milly-Molly-Mandy. "We can have a band, and then we'll recite something. What can we say?"

"Let's write a poem," said little-friend-Susan.

So they thought awhile. And then Milly-Molly-Mandy said:

"Dear Grandpa and Grandma, we want to say
We wish you a happy Golden Wedding Day!"

"Bit long," said Billy Blunt.

"But it rhymes," said Milly-Molly-Mandy.

"Yes, it does," said little-friend-Susan. "Can't we get in something about Many Happy Returns?"

"Can you have returns of Golden Weddings?" asked Milly-Molly-Mandy. "I thought you only had one."

"You could have one every fifty years, I expect," said Billy Blunt. "You'd be a bit old by next time, though!"

"Well, we'd like Grandpa and Grandma to have heaps of Golden Weddings, till they were millions of years old!" said Milly-Molly-Mandy.

So they thought again, and added:

"We want you to know our heart all burns
To wish you Many Happy Returns."

Billy Blunt wrote it down on a piece of paper, and while the others tried to think up some more he went on scribbling for a bit. Then he read out loudly:

"We hope you like this little stunt,
Done by Mister William Blunt!"

There was a lot of shouting at that, as the others of course, wanted to have their names in too! They made so much noise that Mrs Blunt looked in from the corn-shop to see what was up.

Billy Blunt said: "Sorry, Mum!" And they went on with the meeting in whispers.

Well, the great day arrived.

Only a few special people were invited to the party, but there seemed quite a crowd – Grandpa and Grandma, Father and Mother, Uncle and Aunty, Mr Moggs and Mrs Moggs (their nearest neighbours), little-friend-Susan and Baby Moggs (who couldn't be left

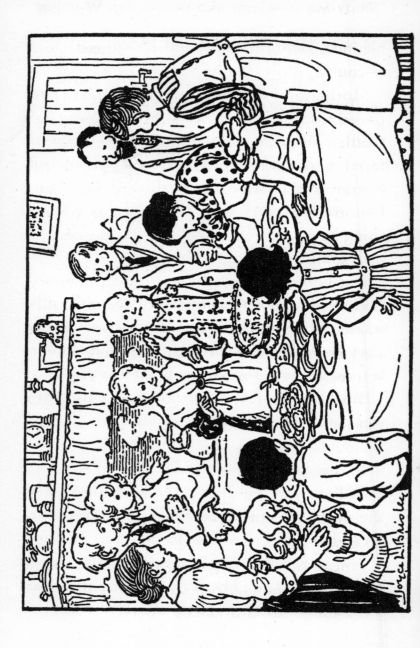

behind), Billy Blunt (by special request), and, of course, Milly-Molly-Mandy.

Mother and Aunty between them had prepared a splendid tea, with the big decorated Golden Wedding cake in the centre, and buttered scones, and brown and white bread-and-butter and honey, and apricot jam, and lemon-curd tarts, and orange buns (everything as nearly golden-coloured as possible, of course) arranged round it.

But before Mother filled the teapot everybody had to give Grandpa and Grandma their golden presents. (Milly-Molly-Mandy and little-friend-Susan and Billy Blunt were all very interested to see what everyone was giving!)

Well, Mr and Mrs Moggs gave a beautiful gilt basket tied with gold ribbons, full of lovely yellow chrysanthemums.

Father and Mother gave a pair of real gold cuff-links to Grandpa, and a little gold locket (with a photo of Milly-Molly-Mandy inside) to Grandma.

Uncle and Aunty gave a gold coin to hang on Grandpa's watch-chain, and a thin gold neck-chain for Grandma's locket.

And then it was time for Milly-Molly-Mandy and little-friend-Susan and Billy Blunt to give their presents.

They stood in a row, and Billy Blunt lifted his shovel-and-poker violin, and Milly-Molly-Mandy her comb-and-tissue-paper mouth-organ, and little-friend-Susan her saucepan-lid clappers; and they played and sang, hummed and clashed, *Happy Birthday to you!* only instead of "birthday" they sang, "Happy Golden Wedding to you!"

And then they shouted their own poem all together:

"Dear Grandpa and Grandma, we want to say
We wish you a happy Golden Wedding Day.
We want you to know our heart all burns
To wish you Many Happy Returns.
We hope you like our little stunt,
From Milly-Molly-Mandy, Susan,
    and Billy Blunt!"

Grandpa and Grandma were nearly over-come, and everybody clapped as the three gave their presents then: two long yellow pencils with brass ends (which looked like gold) from little-friend-Susan; two "Golden-Glamour Sachets" from Billy Blunt; and a little gold bell to ring whenever they wanted her from Milly-Molly-Mandy.

Grandpa and Grandma WERE pleased!

There was quite a bit of talk over Billy Blunt's sachets, though, as he had thought they were scent sachets, but the others said they were shampoos for golden hair, and, of course Grandpa's and Grandma's hair was white!

However, Grandma said her sachet smelled so delicious she would keep it among her handkerchiefs, and Grandpa could do the same with his. So that was all right.

Then they had tea, and Grandpa and Grandma cut big slices of their Golden Wedding cake, with a shiny gilt heart for everybody.

Afterwards Grandpa made quite a long speech. But all Grandma could say was that she thought such a lovely Golden Wedding was well worth waiting fifty years for!

So then Milly-Molly-Mandy and little-friend-Susan and Billy Blunt knew they had really and truly helped in making it such a splendid occasion!

11

MILLY-MOLLY-MANDY
RIDES A HORSE

O<small>NCE</small> <small>UPON</small> <small>A</small> <small>TIME</small> Milly-Molly-Mandy was out playing at horses with little-friend-Susan and Billy Blunt.

There was a clearing in the woods near the nice white cottage with the thatched roof, where Milly-Molly-Mandy lived, and they had found some fallen branches and were galloping astride them along a mossy track.

Then Billy Blunt saw a low-growing branch of a tree which he climbed on, and sat bouncing up and down exactly like real horse-riding. Milly-Molly-Mandy and little-friend-Susan had to stop and watch him, till he let them each have a go.

Then he said firmly, "Now it's my turn." And he got on again and bounced solemnly up and down, while Milly-Molly-Mandy and little-friend-Susan pranced around on their sticks.

(Horse-riding is very good exercise!)

Presently what did they hear but a thud-thudding sound, like real horses' hoofs. And what did they see but five or six real horse-riders come riding along down the mossy track.

"Oh, look!" cried Milly-Molly-Mandy.

"Live horses!" cried little-friend-Susan.

"Mind yourselves!" called Billy Blunt, from his tree.

So they stopped well to one side as the horses passed in single file, hoofs thudding, harnesses creaking, breaths snorting.

Milly-Molly-Mandy and little-friend-Susan
and Billy Blunt hardly looked at the riders, till
one small one in fawn knee-breeches turned
her head and said, "Hullo!" to them.

It was the little girl Jessamine, who lived at
the Big House with the iron railings near the
cross-roads.

"Well!" said Milly-Molly-Mandy, as the
party cantered out into the road towards the
village, "fancy Jessamine having a real horse!"

"Isn't she lucky!" said little-friend-Susan.

"It's the riding school," said Billy Blunt.
"She's learning riding."

Somehow, their pretend-horses didn't seem
quite such fun now. Billy Blunt stopped
bouncing and climbed down.

"I wish we'd got real horses to ride on," said
Milly-Molly-Mandy.

"So do I," said little-friend-Susan.

Billy Blunt said, "Well, what about your old
Twinkletoes?"

"He's Grandpa's pony," said Milly-Molly-
Mandy. "He isn't meant for riding."

"He pulls their market-cart," said little-
friend-Susan.

"Oh, look!" cried Millie Mollie Mandy.

"But he is a horse," said Billy Blunt.

Milly-Molly-Mandy stood and thought.

"I don't believe they'd let us ride him," she said; "but we could *ask*, couldn't we?"

"Oh, *do*!" said little-friend-Susan.

"No harm asking," said Billy Blunt.

So they all ran down the road to the nice white cottage with the thatched roof, into the kitchen, where Mother was busy ironing shirts.

"Oh, Mother!" asked Milly-Molly-Mandy. "Please may we go horse-riding on Twinkletoes?"

"Well, now," said Mother, "you'd better see what Father has to say!"

So they ran outside to the barn, where Father was busy sorting potatoes.

"Father!" asked Milly-Molly-Mandy. "Please may we go horse-riding on Twinkletoes?"

"Why, where do you want to go?" asked Father. "Land's End or John o' Groat's?"

"Oh, no," said Milly-Molly-Mandy (she wasn't sure where either of those places were), "only just in the meadow, perhaps."

"Well, now," said Father, "perhaps you'd better see what Grandpa has to say!"

So they ran around to the stable, where Grandpa was busy mending a broken strap.

"Grandpa!" asked Milly-Molly-Mandy. "Please may we go horse-riding on Twinkle-toes?"

Grandpa didn't answer at once. Then he said slowly:

"Well, you know, he's not exactly used to folks sitting on him, is old Twinkletoes. But we might try!"

So Grandpa tried putting a bridle on Twin-kletoes and strapping an old blanket across his back for a saddle. Then he stooped to lift Milly-Molly-Mandy up.

But Milly-Molly-Mandy said quickly, "Billy Blunt ought to have first go!" (Maybe she wanted to see if Twinkletoes would mind being ridden!)

So Grandpa held the bridle while Billy Blunt got on. And after a moment Twinkletoes clip-clopped slowly across the yard, with Billy Blunt sitting joggling on his back.

They all went into the meadow, and Grand-pa stood by the gate, watching. It was very exciting!

142

"Does it feel nice?" Milly-Molly-Mandy called up to Billy Blunt.

"It looks lovely!" called little-friend-Susan.

"Not bad," returned Billy Blunt. (He was really enjoying it like anything!) "Look out you don't get under his feet!"

They went right across the meadow, and Twinkletoes didn't seem to mind a bit. When they got back to the gate again Billy Blunt slid down, and then Grandpa helped little-friend-Susan up. (Milly-Molly-Mandy had to keep jumping because it was so exciting and so hard to wait her turn! – but of course visitors should have first go.)

Little-friend-Susan only wished that old Twinkletoes wouldn't keep stopping to nibble the grass!

At last Milly-Molly-Mandy's turn came.

She was lifted on to the pony's broad back (it felt awfully high!) and off he went, with Milly-Molly-Mandy holding tight to his mane.

It was terribly thrilling! But soon she was able to sit up and look about a bit. It felt rather like being on a rocking-chair, as Twinkletoes ambled slowly along with his

143

head drooping, while little-friend-Susan picked daisies and Billy Blunt romped with Toby the dog.

Suddenly – what *do* you think? – Twinkletoes seemed to stumble on a rough bit of ground. And next moment Milly-Molly-Mandy slid sprawling over his head down into the long grass!

The others all came running to help her up, Toby the dog barking at poor Twinkletoes, who stood shaking his head in a puzzled sort of way.

"You let his head hang down, didn't you?" said Grandpa; "and he kind of went to sleep! You want to let him feel the reins, only don't pull on them. You'll learn. Up with you, now!"

But Milly-Molly-Mandy wasn't sure she wanted any more riding just at present. "It's Billy's turn again," she said.

But Billy Blunt said, "No! You should always get on at once if you fall off a horse. Go on, get on."

So then Milly-Molly-Mandy got on. And Twinkletoes trotted with her so nicely round the meadow that they all forgot about the tumble.

"Can we have some more rides soon?" asked Milly-Molly-Mandy, as she got down and they all stood patting Twinkletoes.

Grandpa said, Yes, another day, when he had had time to see about some stirrups.

Milly-Molly-Mandy and Billy Blunt and little-friend-Susan were glad to think they had a real horse to ride on now, like the little girl Jessamine!

12

MILLY-MOLLY-MANDY
FINDS A PARCEL

ONCE UPON A TIME Milly-Molly-Mandy walked down to the village with little-friend-Susan, who had to buy some things for her mother at Mr Smale the grocer's shop. (It's always nicer to do that sort of thing with somebody than just by yourself.)

While she waited outside (because there were several people in the shop, so it was rather full) Milly-Molly-Mandy noticed a man, coming along the pavement opposite, stoop as if to pick up something. Then he straightened himself, looked around, and said "Ha Ha!" rather loudly, and walked on.

Milly-Molly-Mandy thought it seemed a bit funny; but grown-ups sometimes did do funny things, so she didn't think more about it. And little-friend-Susan came out just then with a big bag in her arms.

"Let's have a look in Miss Muggins's shop!" said Milly-Molly-Mandy.

So they crossed over and looked in the window (because Miss Muggins sold toys and sweets as well as ladies' things, and it's always fun to see what you might buy if you could!).

But there was nothing new, so they were just going on when Milly-Molly-Mandy said:

"Look! What's this?"

"What's what?" said little-friend-Susan, clutching her bag.

Milly-Molly-Mandy pointed.

"Someone must have dropped it," she said.

It was a neat little parcel tied with string.

Milly-Molly-Mandy bent to pick it up. But – what do you think? – it slid away from her along the pavement! She let out a squeal, and little-friend-Susan dropped an orange from her bag.

But, while picking it up for her, Milly-Molly-Mandy noticed something! Pushing the orange back in the bag, she whispered:

"Susan! don't talk loud, but there's some black cotton tied to that parcel, and I think it goes behind the fence into the Blunts's garden!" Then in her usual voice she said, "We'd best hurry home before you drop any more things, Susan!" – as if quite forgetting what was on the ground.

Then she crept to the fence adjoining Miss Muggins's shop and peeped over. And behind some bushes in the Blunts's garden she could just see a bit of Billy Blunt's leg!

"Ha ha!" she called out (like the man she had watched), "we can see you! You thought you'd had us, didn't you?"

Billy Blunt's grinning face looked round the bush. "So I did," he said, "had you nicely!"

"Can we come in there with you, and watch?" said little-friend-Susan. "There's someone coming along!"

"Hurry up, then, and don't make a lot of row," said Billy Blunt.

So Milly-Molly-Mandy and little-friend-

Susan hurried in at the gate and over to the bushes where Billy Blunt was hiding. And they made themselves as small as possible behind him, while he held the end of his thread and waited.

Young Mrs Rudge the blacksmith's wife, going to see if Miss Muggins sold hair-curlers (she did), stooped to pick up the package. Billy Blunt twitched it away from her, and she called out, "Now, Billy Blunt! – you and your monkey-tricks!" – though she couldn't have seen him!

Then Miss Muggins's Jilly came by with a handful of chocolate-drops (which her aunty must have given her). She nearly trod on the little parcel before she saw it.

Billy Blunt pulled the thread, but Miss Muggins's Jilly's foot was on it, and the cotton broke.

She picked up the package (not noticing the bit of black thread dangling), and, seeing the stamp, supposed it had been dropped by somebody going to the post. So, like a thoughtful little girl, she went and popped it into the letter-box outside Mr Smale the grocer's shop!

"Ohhh!" whispered Milly-Molly-Mandy and little-friend-Susan together, watching from the other side of the fence. "She's posted it!"

Billy Blunt doubled up with silent laughter.

"She never noticed the address – and that it wasn't a proper stamp!"

"What had you put on it?" whispered Milly-Molly-Mandy.

"Mr Nobody, Grand View, The Moon – and a stamp off an old envelope!"

They all nearly burst with laughing, in among the bushes.

"But the postman can't deliver it, so what will he do?" whispered little-friend-Susan.

"He'll have to open it!" Billy Blunt exploded.

"What's inside?" they asked.

"Ssh! – just a stone and a bit of paper with 'Ever been had?'" Billy Blunt said, and set them all off again.

"Oh, but poor Mr Jakes," said Milly-Molly-

Mandy, then, "and he's such a nice postman!
It's too bad to take him in!"

"But I never meant for him to be taken in,"
said Billy Blunt, "and he mustn't ever know
who's done it."

"Can't we do something nice to make up?"
said Milly-Molly-Mandy.

"Send him something nice in a parcel," said
little-friend-Susan.

"Then he might suspect," said Billy Blunt.
"And after all, we didn't post it!"

Miss Muggins's Jilly had gone now, so they
could come out of hiding and laugh all they
wanted, as they couldn't fool anyone else now.
Little-friend-Susan took up her shopping-bag.

But then Milly-Molly-Mandy had a bright
idea.

"Couldn't we get Mr Jakes a proper card
between us, and post it to him? We needn't
sign it."

They all counted their pennies, and then
they went to look at Miss Muggins's greeting
cards. The prettiest said, 'To my husband' –
but Mr Jakes might think Mrs Jakes had sent
it! Another (cheaper) said, 'To my Friend'.

And they decided on that.

Billy Blunt wrote the name and address with his pen, and they bought a real stamp, and posted the card in the letter-box (though Mr Jakes lived only next door).

And then Milly-Molly-Mandy and little-friend-Susan ran home.

Well! – you can guess how pleased and surprised Mr Jakes the postman was to have to deliver such a nice card to himself! But, actually, it was Miss Crisp the postmistress who found Billy Blunt's little package. And she saw it was just a bit of nonsense, and threw it away!

13

MILLY-MOLLY-MANDY
GOES EXCAVATING

ONCE UPON A TIME, as Milly-Molly-Mandy was going into school, she noticed a number of young men come striding along from the cross-roads and up Hooker's Hill. They were carrying spades and pickaxes and things, but somehow they didn't look like men who were mending the roads.

"I wonder what they're going to do," said Milly-Molly-Mandy.

"They're going to do excavating," said Billy Blunt. "I heard my dad talking about it. They've got permission."

"What's excavating?"

"Digging up old things," said Billy Blunt.

"Like buried treasure? That sort of thing? How do they know where to do it?"

"They guess," said Billy Blunt. "They guess Ancient Britons might have lived up there once. They just want to find out."

It sounded rather exciting. Milly-Molly-Mandy wished she could go digging instead of just going to school!

Next Saturday morning she took Toby the dog for a walk down to the village, rather hoping to hear more about the excavating. As she passed the corn-shop she saw Billy Blunt hanging over the side-gate.

"Hullo!" said Milly-Molly-Mandy. "What are you doing?"

Billy Blunt didn't answer. (Anyone could

see he was doing nothing.) But after a moment he said:

"Want to see something?"

Of course Milly-Molly-Mandy said yes, at once.

And Billy Blunt drew his hand slowly out of his pocket and opened it. There was a flat, round thing in it, streaked brown and green.

"What d'you make of that?" he asked.

"What is it? Is it money? Where did you find it?"

"I excavated it."

"You didn't! Where?"

"In our garden. By the bonfire heap. I was just digging a bit, to see if there might be any-thing – you never know – and I dug this up."

"It must be ancient!" said Milly-Molly-Mandy. "Have you shown it t anybody?"

"Not yet." Billy Blunt ru ed it carefully with his handkerchief. "Mother's busy, and Dad's got customers."

"Let's show it to Mr Rudge!" said Milly-Molly-Mandy. "He knows about iron and such things; he'll know if it's valuable."

So they went along to the forge, where the

blacksmith was blowing up his fire.

Milly-Molly-Mandy peeped in the doorway. "Mr Rudge! Billy Blunt's excavated something!" she told him. "And we want to know if you think it's very valuable!"

The blacksmith looked round with a twinkle in his eye. He held out one great grimy hand, working the bellows with the other, and Billy Blunt put the precious coin into it.

Mr Rudge examined it one side, then the other. Then he rubbed it on his big leather apron and looked again.

"Hmmm," he said solemnly. "Georgian, I'd say. Yes. Undoubtedly."

"Is that very ancient?" asked Milly-Molly-Mandy.

"What's it worth?" asked Billy Blunt.

"If you're asking me, don't you take a ha'penny less than a penny for it. But mind you," he added, "if it's treasure-trove it may belong to the Crown."

He gave the coin back and turned again to his fire. Billy Blunt and Milly-Molly-Mandy came out into the sunshine, looking to see what all that rubbing had done.

"Looks like there's a head –" said Billy Blunt; "can't see any date."

"What's treasure-trove mean?" asked Milly-Molly-Mandy.

"Dunno. P'raps if you dig up treasure you aren't supposed to keep it."

Then Milly-Molly-Mandy had an idea.

"If you dug this out of your garden maybe there's some more there! Can't you go excavating again? I'll help."

So they went back to the Blunts's garden, beside the corn-shop, and Billy Blunt led the

"It's awfully hard under here . . . "

way round the rhubarb-bed to the end by the rubbish-heap and the bonfire.

He picked up a trowel and handed Milly-Molly-Mandy a rusty knife to dig with, and they began jabbing about in the earth and weeds. But there didn't seem to be anything else but stones. (Plenty of them.)

Presently Milly-Molly-Mandy said:

"It's awfully hard under here – feels like rock."

"Where?" said Billy Blunt. He came over and used his trowel. "Looks like cement."

"Perhaps it's buried treasure cemented in!" said Milly-Molly-Mandy.

"Fetch a spade out of the shed there," ordered Billy Blunt. "Hurry!"

So Milly-Molly-Mandy ran and fetched him a spade, and she took over the trowel. And they could see there was something, underneath the earth and weeds!

"It's got an iron lid!" panted Milly-Molly-Mandy.

"It's an iron chest, cemented down!" puffed Billy Blunt.

They got the top scraped clear. It was square and rusty, with a kind of loop to lift it by.

"This is buried treasure all right!"

Billy Blunt was red with excitement.

Milly-Molly-Mandy wanted to jump and shout, but she was too busy.

The lid was awfully heavy. They tried to lever it up, but they couldn't.

"You'll have to tell your father and mother, won't you?" said Milly-Molly-Mandy, at last.

Billy Blunt dropped the spade and dashed indoors. And presently Mr Blunt came out, in his apron, and walked over to their hole.

He took one look.

"*That?*" he said. "Whatever will you be up to next? That's only the cover of the drain!" When he could stop laughing he added, "Just as well you unearthed it, though – there might have been trouble if the authorities knew it had got covered over. Don't know how it happened."

"But look, Dad. I found this –" Billy Blunt showed his piece of money. "We thought there might be some more. It's quite ancient, isn't it? The blacksmith said Georgian."

Mr Blunt scraped with his pocket knife a moment. Then he fished a few coins from his trousers' pocket, picked out a penny and handed it over with the other. "There's your same Georgian coin," he chuckled, "King George V – only a bit cleaner. Yours looks as if it's been on the bonfire!"

Well! It was all very disappointing. But anyhow, those two pennies bought two fine peppermint humbugs from Miss Muggins's shop. And, sucking away together, Billy Blunt and Milly-Molly-Mandy both agreed it had really been quite fun while it lasted.

But they hoped the excavators up on Hooker's Hill were having better luck!

14

MILLY-MOLLY-MANDY

HAS AN ADVENTURE

ONCE UPON A TIME, one Saturday afternoon, Milly-Molly-Mandy had quite an
adventure.

There was a special children's film showing
at the cinema in the next village, and Milly-
Molly-Mandy and little-friend-Susan were
going to it, by bus, quite by themselves!

"Keep together, and don't talk to strangers,"
said Mother, giving Milly-Molly-Mandy the
money for the cinema and for the bus, there
and back.

"But supposing strangers speak to us?" said
Milly-Molly-Mandy.

"Always answer politely," said Mother, "but
no more than that."

So Milly-Molly-Mandy set off from the nice

163

white cottage with the thatched roof, down the road with the hedges each side to the Moggs's cottage where little-friend-Susan was waiting for her. And they walked on together to the cross-roads, feeling very important, to catch the bus.

There was plenty of time, but they thought they had better run the last part of the way, to be on the safe side. But nobody was waiting at the cross-roads, so they wondered if they had missed the bus after all.

Then one or two people came up and waited, so it couldn't have gone. And presently it came in sight.

And just as everybody was getting on who do you suppose came along and got on too? – Why, Billy Blunt!

Milly-Molly-Mandy and little-friend-Susan took their seats and paid their half-fares, and pocketed the change carefully (three pennies for Milly-Molly-Mandy, a threepenny piece for little-friend-Susan). And then they sat looking out of the windows to make sure they didn't get carried past the cinema.

Billy Blunt had made for a seat right in

front, looking as if he were quite used to doing this sort of thing by himself. (But he couldn't have been, really!) He managed to be first to get off the moment the bus stopped, so they didn't actually see if he went into the cinema.

Inside, it was so dark you couldn't recognize anybody. Milly-Molly-Mandy and little-friend-Susan held hands tight, not to lose one another.

It was all very exciting.

And so was the film. They wished it needn't end. When it was all over it seemed funny to come out into daylight again and find the same ordinary world outside.

They saw Billy Blunt coming away, talking with another boy. So they walked straight to the bus-stop and began waiting. (The bus ran every hour, and if one had just gone they might be a long time getting home.)

Suddenly little-friend-Susan said loudly, "My money!" and began rummaging in her coat-pocket.

Milly-Molly-Mandy said, "Why? Where?" and began rummaging in her own. (But her three pennies were safe all right.)

165

"My threepenny piece!" said little-friend-Susan; "I had it here..."

She looked in her right-hand pocket, then in her left, then in her hands. Then Milly-Molly-Mandy looked.

Then they looked on the pavement, and in the gutter.

"You must have dropped it in the cinema, Susan," said Milly-Molly-Mandy. "Let's go back and ask."

"But I didn't," said little-friend-Susan. "I felt it in my pocket as we came out."

So they looked all along the pavement. But still they couldn't find it.

"Well, we've just got to walk home," said Milly-Molly-Mandy, at last. "You can't go by yourself. We'll have to walk together."

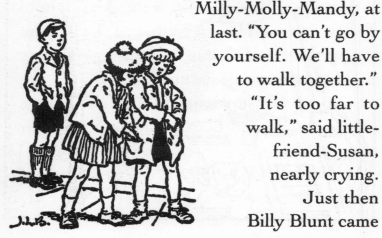

"It's too far to walk," said little-friend-Susan, nearly crying.

Just then Billy Blunt came

"She's lost her money!"

up to join the queue. Milly-Molly-Mandy said to him, "She's lost her money!"

Billy Blunt didn't know what to say, so he said nothing.

A gypsy woman standing near with a baby and big basket said, "There now! Lost your money, have you, ducks?"

Milly-Molly-Mandy said again, "We've got to walk home."

Billy Blunt said, "It's too far." Then he said, "Here, have mine. I'll manage."

But Milly-Molly-Mandy and little-friend-Susan said together, "You can't walk that far all by yourself!"

The gypsy woman began fumbling under her apron for her purse.

"I may have just a spare copper or two," she said. "Where does the little lady live? I'll call on her ma, and she can pay me back some day!"

Milly-Molly-Mandy, remembering what Mother had said, answered politely, "No, thank you very much!" – when at that moment the bus came in sight.

"Here!" said Billy Blunt, holding out his money.

Milly-Molly-Mandy and little-friend-Susan
didn't like to take it. They couldn't think what
to do.

An old truck laden
with empty cans and
things was coming
rattling down the
road. It overtook the bus
and was just clattering past the
bus-stop when Milly-Molly-Mandy suddenly
started waving her arms wildly at it.

"Cyril, stop! Cyril!" she shouted.

The truck slowed down, and a tousled head
looked back from the driver's seat.

"It's Cyril!" Milly-Molly-Mandy told the
others, excitedly. "He drives things to the station for Uncle sometimes!" She ran forward.
"Oh, Cyril! May I ride home with you?" she
asked.

"You may not," said Cyril. "In that get-up? —
I'd have your ma after me. Anyhow, I'm not
going by your house today — only to the cross-
roads."

Little-friend-Susan pulled at Milly-Molly-
Mandy's sleeve.

"But, Milly-Molly-Mandy! You know we've got to keep together!"

The bus was drawing up. People were beginning to get on.

Billy Blunt asked Cyril quickly, "Can you take me?"

"If you want," said Cyril. "But hop on quick."

The bus was tooting for him to get out of the way.

Billy Blunt pushed his money at little-friend-Susan, saying, "Go on – hurry!" Then he clambered into the truck beside Cyril, helped by Cyril's very grubby hand, and off they went rattling down the road.

"Now then, you two!" the bus-driver called out of his small side-window, "are you coming with us or aren't you? We haven't got all day, you know."

And Milly-Molly-Mandy and little-friend-Susan (full of smiles) rushed to scramble on to the bus. And off they went, after the truck, down the road, and along the winding leafy lanes.

Billy Blunt was waiting at the cross-roads to

see them arrive. He looked quite pleased with himself! (He had an oily smear down one leg, and his hands were black.)

"I got here quicker than you did," was all he said, when they thanked him.

And — do you know! — that threepenny piece of little-friend-Susan's was found, after all!

It had worked through a small hole in her coat-pocket down into the lining. And she was able to work it out again and pay Billy Blunt back the next day.

15

MILLY-MOLLY-MANDY
ON BANK HOLIDAY

ONCE UPON A TIME, one fine day, Milly-Molly-Mandy couldn't think what to do with herself.

It felt as if something specially nice should be done, as it was a Bank Holiday. But Father and Mother and Grandpa and Grandma and Uncle and Aunty all said they were busy, and everywhere would be so crowded today, and they preferred to stay at home.

"Why not go and play with little-friend-Susan?" said Mother, getting out jam-pots ready for jam-making.

"Get yourself some sweets, if the shop's open," said Father, feeling in his trousers' pocket.

So Milly-Molly-Mandy called to Toby the

dog and wandered down the
road with the hedges each
side, to the Moggs's cottage.

Little-friend-Susan was outside, minding her baby sister.
They both had clean
frocks and their hats on.

"Hullo, Milly-Molly-
Mandy!" said little-
friend-Susan. "It's Bank
Holiday today. Father's
going to take us all out on
the red bus. I wish you were coming too!"

So did Milly-Molly-Mandy. But as she
wasn't she called to Toby the dog and wandered on down to the village.

Miss Muggins's shop had its blind half-
down over the toys and sweets in the window.
But Milly-Molly-Mandy tried the handle, just
in case, and Miss Muggins's Jilly peeped
through the collarettes and gloves hanging
across the glass of the door.

When she saw who was there Miss
Muggins's Jilly stooped and said through the
letter-box slit:

"We aren't open today, Milly-Molly-Mandy. It's Bank Holiday. My aunty's taking me to my granny's, by the red bus.

(Toby the dog was so surprised at a voice coming from the letter-box that he barked and barked!)

But next moment the door was unlocked, and Miss Muggins's Jilly (in her best white hat) stepped outside, followed by Miss Muggins herself (in her best black).

As she locked the door behind her and put the key in her bag Miss Muggins said:

"Good morning, Milly-Molly-Mandy. Now we mustn't delay, or we shall miss the bus."

And Milly-Molly-Mandy, holding Toby the dog, watched them go hurrying down to the cross-roads, where several people were standing waiting.

The red bus arrived just as Mr Moggs, carrying the baby, and Mrs Moggs, with little-friend-Susan, came running and waving by the short-cut across the fields, only *just* in time. Everybody scrambled aboard; the bus gave a "ping!" and off they all went, away into the distance.

"Hullo!" he said, grinning

And you wouldn't believe how empty the village felt!

There was only Mr Smale the grocer (in his shirtsleeves) reading a newspaper at his doorway, and Milly-Molly-Mandy standing with Toby the dog, wondering what to do next.

There didn't seem to be anything.

Then, round the corner by the forge, who should come along but Billy Blunt, carrying an old rusty tea-tray under his arm!

"Hullo!" he said, grinning.

"Hullo!" said Milly-Molly-Mandy, rather dolefully. "It's Bank Holiday today."

"I know," said Billy Blunt. "And I mean to have one. You can come along if you want."

"Where to?" asked Milly-Molly-Mandy. "What are you going to do? What's that thing?"

"It's a tea-tray," said Billy Blunt. "I found it on Mr Rudge's junk-heap. I shall put it back when I've done. Come on if you're coming."

So, feeling very curious, Milly-Molly-Mandy and Toby the dog followed him.

They walked to the cross-roads, then up the steep hilly road beyond. Presently they climbed a low fence and through a lot of brambles and things, till they came out on a high meadow looking down on the village.

"Here's the place," said Billy Blunt.

And he solemnly placed his tray on the ground and sat on it. And with a few shoves and pushes he went sliding down over the grass, faster and faster down the bank, leaving Milly-Molly-Mandy and Toby the dog shouting and barking behind him, till at last he came to a stop by the hedge at the bottom of the meadow.

"How's that?" he said triumphantly, as he climbed panting back to the top again, dragging the tray. "Want a go? You have to mind out for the nettles by the hedge..."

So Milly-Molly-Mandy sat on the tray, and Billy Blunt gave her a good shove. And off she went down the bank, with the wind in her hair and Toby the dog racing alongside, till she spilled over in the long grass just short of the nettles.

177

Then Billy Blunt took several more turns till he was quite out of breath, and Milly-Molly-Mandy had another go.

They only stopped at last because it began to feel like dinner-time. They were very hungry and very warm (and rather grubby too!).

"Well!" said Milly-Molly-Mandy, as they started homeward, "this is a proper Bank Holiday, isn't it?"

"Well," said Billy Blunt, "I think Bank Holidays are meant so that people in banks can stop counting up their money. It's not this sort of bank really, you know."

"This is the sort of Bank Holiday I like best, anyhow," said Milly-Molly-Mandy.

16

MILLY-MOLLY-MANDY
DOES AN ERRAND

ONCE UPON A TIME Milly-Molly-Mandy
went on an errand to the village. (It was only
to get a tin of cocoa which Mother had forgot-
ten to order.)

When she came to the grocer's shop
Mr Smale the grocer was outside
his door, opening up a box of
kippers. (Kippers do smell
rather kippery, so Milly-
Molly-Mandy guessed
Mr Smale preferred to
keep them outside –
where people passing
could see them too: he didn't
often sell kippers.)

179

While Milly-Molly-Mandy waited till he had done, someone came out of the baker's shop next door, carrying a heavy shopping-basket and an umbrella, as well as a loaf of bread.

It was one of the Miss Thumbles, who lived in a cottage by the duck-pond. There were two Miss Thumbles, sisters, both so alike that the only way Milly-Molly-Mandy could tell them apart was that one always seemed to wear a hat, even to go in the garden. That was Miss Thumble. The other one, of course, was the Other Miss Thumble.

But today, being rather cold and windy, this Miss Thumble wore a warm woolly scarf tied over her grey hair. So Milly-Molly-Mandy really couldn't be sure whether she were Miss Thumble or the Other Miss Thumble.

Seeing the newly opened box of kippers, Miss Thumble (or perhaps it was the Other Miss Thumble) stopped and said:

"Dear me! I should like a couple of those – my sister does enjoy a nice grilled kipper for her tea! But how I'm going to manage to carry everything..."

Mr Smale quickly clapped two flat glistening brown kippers together and went into the shop to wrap them up. So Milly-Molly-Mandy said:

"Shall I carry your bread for you?"

And she took it, while Miss Thumble thankfully put her basket down on the step to find her purse, and went inside to pay.

As Milly-Molly-Mandy waited there, with the loaf of bread and the basket, who should look over the Blunts's garden gate opposite but Billy Blunt! He came out and strolled across the road, hands in pockets.

"Hullo! That's not your basket," said Billy Blunt.

"No," said Milly-Molly-Mandy. "It's Miss Thumble's. I'm helping to carry her things."

"You can't carry that," said Billy Blunt.

"Yes, I can," said Milly-Molly-Mandy. "Some of it."

"It's too heavy," said Billy Blunt.

Milly-Molly-Mandy rather hoped he was going to offer to help too. But he only turned and went back in at the garden gate, just as Miss Thumble came out of the shop.

She thanked Milly-Molly-Mandy for

keeping an eye on her basket, and tried to find room in it for the parcel of kippers. But one thing and another kept falling out – potatoes and cheese and a big round cabbage – rolling about on the pavement.

Milly-Molly-Mandy picked them up, very nearly dropping the loaf at the same time.

"Here, give 'em here," said Billy Blunt.

He had come out again, pulling his little old box-on-wheels with him.

Putting the heavy basket into it, with all the odd potatoes and kippers and things, he set off hauling it along the road, past the forge and round by the duck-pond, Milly-Molly-Mandy following hugging the loaf, and Miss Thumble stumping after them looking as pleased as anything!

By the little cottages they stopped, and Miss Thumble rattled the letter-box of one. And presently the door opened; and there was the other Miss Thumble, wearing felt slippers *and* a hat. (So Milly-Molly-Mandy knew *she* must be Miss Thumble, and the first one was the Other Miss Thumble.)

They all helped to pile the things on to the kitchen table, and both the Miss Thumbles were very grateful at having so much kind help.

"I know my sister finds the shopping very heavy at times," said Miss Thumble.

"But I don't usually have quite so much to carry all at once!" said the Other Miss Thumble.

She opened one of the packages for her sister to offer the visitors each a biscuit before they left. And though Billy Blunt wasn't too keen on oatmeal biscuits he took one and said thank-you nicely, and so did Milly-Molly-Mandy. (She liked all kinds of biscuits – but some more than others, of course!)

They walked, munching together, back with the empty cart as far as the Blunts's gate.

Billy Blunt said, "We'd better see if they'd like us to carry their shopping for them other times."

183

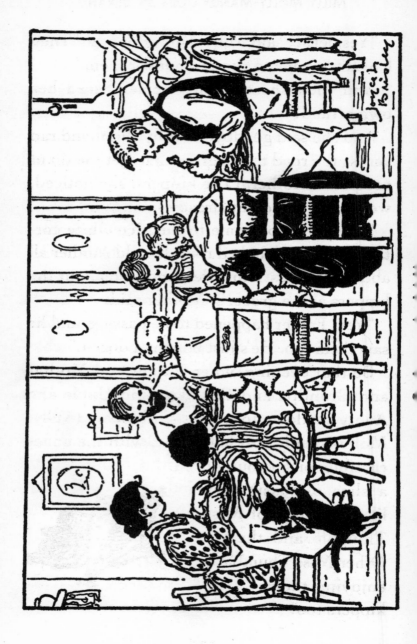

"Yes, let's!" said Milly-Molly-Mandy. "They haven't anyone to run errands for them."

And then she suddenly remembered her own errand!

And she said goodbye to Billy Blunt and ran across the road to the grocer's to get the tin of cocoa for Mother. (The kippers, she noticed, were nearly sold out already.)

When she got home to the nice white cottage with the thatched roof she told Mother all about the Miss Thumbles, and also about the kippers at the grocer's. Mother said:

"Yes! Father happened to be passing, and he saw them too. He's just bought a dozen."

So that evening, when Father and Mother and Grandpa and Grandma and Uncle and Aunty sat down to enjoy their kippers (Milly-Molly-Mandy had half a one, with the bones carefully picked out, on a slice of toast) they liked to think of Miss Thumble and the Other Miss Thumble enjoying their kippers too!

17

MILLY-MOLLY-MANDY
AND A WET DAY

ONCE UPON A TIME, one morning, when
Milly-Molly-Mandy went off to school, it was
raining and raining. (But she had on her rubber boots and raincoat and hood.)

When she got to the Moggs's cottage there
was little-friend-Susan (in rubber boots
and raincoat and hood) watching for her at
the door.

"Oh, what a nasty wet, rainy day!" said
little-friend-Susan, running out to join her.

"Mother says, if we keep going it won't
hurt," said Milly-Molly-Mandy.

So they kept going, trudging along together
down the wet road with the wet hedges each
side, very glad to have each other to squeal to
when the cold raindrops dripped off their noses.

When they got to the duck-pond all the
little ducks were flapping and
quacking away as if quite
enjoying such a nice
wet, rainy day!
When they got to
the village Billy
Blunt (in thick
shoes and raincoat)
was dashing from the corn-shop; and Miss
Muggins's niece Jilly (in new red rubber
boots and her mackintosh over her head) was
running from the draper's shop. They hadn't
far to go, of course, but Milly-Molly-Mandy
and little-friend-Susan arrived at school
almost the same time, together with some
other boys and girls who came by the red bus
to the crossroads.

They all hung up their coats and hats and
changed their shoes, flapping and quacking
away together like a lot of little ducks, as if
they too quite enjoyed the rainy day! (Milly-
Molly-Mandy and little-friend-Susan were
dry and warm as toast after their long walk.)

When morning school was over the rain had

stopped for a bit. But everywhere was still sopping wet, and in the road outside the school gate was a great muddy puddle.

Milly-Molly-Mandy, and a few others who went home for dinner (some who lived a long way off ate theirs at school), rather enjoyed having to wade through. Billy Blunt chose the deepest place. But Miss Muggins's Jilly, who tried to jump over, made a fine splash.

"It's a good thing we've got our mackintoshes on!" said Milly-Molly-Mandy.

"We ought to be ducks!" said little-friend-Susan.

"Road ought to be mended," said Billy Blunt.

He looked around and picked up some stones which he threw into the puddle. Milly-Molly-Mandy threw in a few bits of broken slate, and little-friend-Susan a handful of leaves and twigs. But it didn't make much difference.

"You'll get yourselves muddy," said Miss Muggins's Jilly.

"We need more stuff," said Billy Blunt.

So they looked about in hedges and ditches, picking up anything to throw in.

Miss Muggins's Filly . . . tried to jump over

"Put 'em just here," said Billy Blunt. "No sense throwing them all over the place."

"I think I'd better go in now," said Miss Muggins's Jilly. "My aunty wouldn't like me to get my new rubber boots wet."

"I thought that's what rubber boots were for," said Milly-Molly-Mandy.

"They're wet already, anyhow," said little-friend-Susan.

"Don't stand there jabbering," said Billy Blunt. "Get busy, or get out of the way."

So Miss Muggins's Jilly went off home. But Milly-Molly-Mandy and little-friend-Susan and Billy Blunt carried on, looking for things to throw into the puddle.

They found some nice bits of brick on the waste ground by the crossroads. Also a splendid lump of broken paving-stone; but it was too heavy to carry, and they had to leave it after a struggle.

Then they had to hurry home to their dinners, and Milly-Molly-Mandy (with farthest to go) only *just* wasn't late for hers.

As soon as she could she hurried back to school, little-friend-Susan joining her on the way. But Billy Blunt was there already, adding fresh stones to mend the roadway. He had his box-on-wheels beside him.

"I got an idea while I was eating my pudding," said Billy Blunt. "We ought to be able to fetch that bit of paving-stone in this!"

So, with the little cart rattling and bumping along between them, they ran across the waste ground by the crossroads.

And together they heaved and they pushed and they grunted, till they got the stone out of the long grass, on to the little cart.

And then they pulled and they pushed, and they grunted, till they got it wheeled over the rough ground into the roadway.

And then they heaved and they grunted (which always seems to help!) till they slid the stone out into the middle of the puddle, with a fine muddy *splosh*!

"That's done it!" said Billy Blunt with satisfaction, wiping himself with some grass.

And then the bell rang, and they had to scurry in and tidy up.

When school was over everyone used the stepping-stones as they left, and kept dry and clean.

Then – what do you think? – as the bus that took some of the children home stopped for them at the crossroads a grey-haired lady got off, and came down to the school gate.

She asked Milly-Molly-Mandy, who was standing nearest:

"Has Miss Edwards come out yet? Would you mind telling her her mother's here?"

Milly-Molly-Mandy was surprised. (She had never thought of Teacher as having a mother!) Miss Edwards came hurrying out, very pleased, to welcome the visitor and take her into her own cottage next door. And they both used the stepping-stones and were glad

to find the road had been so nicely mended –
because Mrs Edwards hadn't any rubber
boots on, only lady's shoes and an umbrella.

"Well, now!" said Mother, when Milly-
Molly-Mandy came running home to the nice
white cottage with the thatched roof. "What
have you been up to? Have you got wet?"

"No!" said Milly-Molly-Mandy. "We kept
going, like you said, and I'm warm as anything!"

18

MILLY-MOLLY-MANDY

MAKES SOME TOFFEE

ONCE UPON A TIME Milly-Molly-Mandy
with little-friend-Susan and Billy Blunt were
in the village, planning how to spend their
pennies to get the most sweets.

Miss Muggins's shop had the usual jars of
raspberry drops
and aniseed
balls; Mr Smale
the grocer's
had coconut
ice and
caramels.

"But they
go so quickly,"
said Milly-
Molly-Mandy.

"And they're expensive," said little-friend-Susan.

"Sugar's cheaper," said Billy Blunt, his nose to the glass, "but not so interesting."

"Mother makes toffee sometimes, with sugar," said Milly-Molly-Mandy. "I wonder if we could!"

"How does your mother make it?" asked little-friend-Susan.

"She puts sugar, and butter, and some vinegar, in a frying-pan, and boils it up," said Milly-Molly-Mandy.

"Vinegar!" said Billy Blunt. "Can't be nice."

"It is then!" said Milly-Molly-Mandy. "It's lovely!"

"Well, why don't we buy sugar, and ask if we can make some ourselves?" said little-friend-Susan.

"If you think you know how," said Billy Blunt. "Don't want to waste things."

So they all went into the shop and put their pennies on the counter, and Mr Smale the grocer weighed out sugar and handed it over. And they ran all the way to the nice white cottage with the thatched roof (where Milly-

Molly-Mandy lived), into the kitchen where Mother was busy cooking.

"Mother!" said Milly-Molly-Mandy. "May we make toffee all by ourselves? We've bought some sugar."

"Yes," said Billy Blunt.

"Please," said little-friend-Susan.

Mother said: "Very well. You may use the stove after dinner, directly the washing-up is done, and I won't watch you!"

So, soon after dinner, Billy Blunt and little-friend-Susan came running round again.

Milly-Molly-Mandy was all ready for them. Mother was at her sewing-machine, but she only glanced up to say hullo.

"You won't take any notice of us, will you, Mother?" said Milly-Molly-Mandy.

"No! I'm too busy," said Mother.

So they set to work.

They tipped their sugar into the frying-pan, with a knob of butter and a spoonful of water to start it melting. Milly-Molly-Mandy stirred with a wooden spoon, little-friend-Susan found a dish for the toffee, and Billy Blunt greased it well.

"You don't really put vinegar in it, do you?" he said.

"You do, don't you, Mother?" said Milly-Molly-Mandy.

The sewing-machine stopped a moment. "I usually add a small spoonful, to lessen the sweetness," said Mother. "There's some in the larder." And the machine rattled on again.

So Billy Blunt fetched the bottle, and they measured a spoonful into the pan.

"We have to try some in cold water to see when it's done," said Milly-Molly-Mandy. (She always liked that part!)

So little-friend-Susan fetched a cupful, and they dripped a few drops in off the spoon. But it only made the water look dirty.

"It goes in hard balls when it's done," said Milly-Molly-Mandy.

"Then it isn't done," said Billy Blunt.

"It hasn't boiled properly," said little-friend-Susan.

Presently Mother said:

"There's rather an odd smell, isn't there?"

"You promised not to watch us!" said Milly-Molly-Mandy.

"I'm not watching," said Mother, "but I can't help smelling."

"It's the vinegar," said Billy Blunt.

"P'raps it's getting done," said little-friend-Susan.

So they tried a bit more in cold water. It tasted odd, but not done.

Presently Father came in from working in his vegetable garden.

"Hullo? What's going on here?" he asked, sniffing.

"We're making toffee!" said Milly-Molly-Mandy.

"All by ourselves!" said little-friend-Susan.

"We bought our own sugar," said Billy Blunt.

"What's the flavouring?" asked Father. "Onion?" He got his seed labels from the mantelshelf and went out again.

They all laughed. Fancy onion in toffee! All the same – "It does smell sort of funny," said Milly-Molly-Mandy.

"P'raps the pan was oniony?" said little-friend-Susan.

"No!" said Mother, over her shoulder.

"It's that vinegar,"
said Billy Blunt, again.

Suddenly Mother asked:
"Do you always read
labels carefully when you
cook? It's one of the first
rules."

"I read that bottle," said Billy Blunt. "It said
vinegar." And he brought the bottle to show
her.

The label read – *Garlic Vinegar!*

"*Ohhh!*" exclaimed Milly-Molly-Mandy and
little-friend-Susan, loudly.

Mother dropped her sewing.

"I should have remembered there were two
sorts of vinegar in the larder," she said, "but I
so seldom use that smaller bottle. I wonder if
you can cover up with some other flavour,
peppermint perhaps?"

She found a tiny bottle in the cupboard.

So (reading the label with great care) they
added a few drops of peppermint essence to
the toffee, before turning it out into the
greased dish to cool before cutting it up.

The rest of the afternoon they played down

by the stream, with Toby the dog. And, do you know, they all thought the toffee wasn't really so bad! (Father said he had never tasted better garlic-toffee!) And it certainly lasted them a long while.

But I don't fancy they will make any more like it – they read labels very carefully now!

19

MILLY-MOLLY-MANDY
HAS AMERICAN VISITORS

ONCE UPON A TIME Milly-Molly-Mandy felt rather excited.

Aunty had a letter with a foreign stamp on from her brother Tom, saying that he and his wife and children were coming over from America to visit their English relatives.

Aunty had not seen her brother Tom since he was quite young, and had never seen his wife, or their children, though they and Milly-Molly-Mandy had exchanged letters and paper dolls.

"Will Sallie and Lallie and Buddy come to

stay here?" asked Milly-Molly-Mandy. "Where will they sleep?"

"We must think," said Mother. "Your Uncle Tom and Aunty Sadie will have the spare room, of course, and Sallie and Lallie might squeeze together in your little room. Perhaps we can make up a bed on the floor for Buddy beside his parents."

"But where will I sleep?" asked Milly-Molly-Mandy.

"You'll have to have a little floor-bed too, beside Father and me," said Mother.

Milly-Molly-Mandy thought that sounded rather fun. (Certainly nicer than wandering around all night with nowhere to sleep!)

"It won't be for long," said Aunty, folding up her letter, "there are other relatives to visit."

Then everybody in the nice white cottage with the thatched roof got very busy. Father picked some of his best fruit and vegetables; Mother made lots of pies and cakes; and Grandpa groomed Twinkletoes and washed the pony-trap; Grandma crocheted a fine new tea-cosy; Uncle collected plenty of eggs from his chickens; Aunty cleaned and polished all the rooms; and Milly-Molly-Mandy helped where she could, and was very useful indeed.

When she told Billy Blunt about it, he grinned and said:

"You'll have to learn to talk American, now!" (Which set Milly-Molly-Mandy wondering, until she remembered how she and Sallie and Lallie and Buddy had written to each other in English!)

Well, the important day came.

Uncle and Aunty went by bus to the railway station, to meet the train. And Grandpa, with Milly-Molly-Mandy and Twinkletoes and the pony-trap, went to meet the bus at the cross-roads as it returned, to drive Sallie and Lallie and Buddy and their mother and the luggage home.

There wasn't room in the pony-trap for everybody. So Uncle and Aunty and Milly-Molly-Mandy all walked home together with Uncle Tom, through the village and along the road with hedges each side.

Uncle Tom looked round about him, saying "Well, this sure is a bit of the old country!" as they went.

When Milly-Molly-Mandy showed him the corn-shop where Billy Blunt lived, and the Moggs's cottage where little-friend-Susan lived, Uncle Tom said, "You don't say!" (though she had just said it!).

When they came to the nice white cottage with the thatched roof Uncle Tom said, "Well, this sure looks a picture!" (though it just looked like home to Milly-Molly-Mandy).

The new Aunty Sadie was helping Mother and Grandma and Aunty in the kitchen, when they got in, and Sallie and Lallie and Buddy were running about, all chattering together, and it all sounded very exciting!

The grown-ups sat down at the big table, and the young ones had a small table to themselves (there wasn't room for everybody otherwise).

They talked about the big boat they had come over on, and about the big place they had come from (which was America, of course), and Uncle Tom told stories of Indians and horse-riding and deserts, and it was all terribly exciting!

They didn't a bit want to go to bed at bedtime.

But that was exciting too, going to bed in new places – Sallie and Lallie in Milly-Molly-Mandy's little attic room, Buddy in a make-shift bed in the spare room, and Milly-Molly-Mandy herself on a mattress on the floor in Father's and Mother's room.

She lay listening to the grown-ups' talk rumbling on and on downstairs, until at last she fell asleep, and it was morning again.

After breakfast they went out to play in the yard, and Milly-Molly-Mandy showed her cousins the old tumbledown pigsty. (It was quite clean and empty, no pigs lived in it now.)

"This is my house," said Milly-Molly-Mandy, "but you can come inside. We must shut the gate, to keep the lions out."

"You don't have lions," said Buddy.

"Oh, we do!" said Milly-Molly-Mandy. "There's one now! Quick! Hurry! Hurry!"

And they all rushed squealing into the pigsty, as Toby the dog came capering up to see what was going on. Milly-Molly-Mandy held the broken gate shut.

"We can't come out till he goes away," she said, "he might eat us!"

Presently Toby the dog went off to see what was moving round by the shed, and they all crept out to gather up a few windfall apples so that they wouldn't starve!

They were just hurrying back with them to the sty, when they heard a frightful hooting noise. And a strange figure came leaping towards them.

(It was Billy Blunt with an old sack over one shoulder and a chicken's tail-feather stuck in his hair!)

"It's Indians! Run! Run!" shrieked Milly-Molly-Mandy.

And they all rushed screaming back into the sty and pushed the gate to, only *just* in time!

"You know, I think he may be quite a kind

They all rushed screaming back into the sty

Indian, really," said Milly-Molly-Mandy, then. "Would you like an apple?" And she held out a nice one over the gate.

"Wah!" said Billy Blunt, taking and biting it.

So they let him come in. And they all huddled together in the pigsty, eating windfall apples (to keep themselves from starving), and throwing the cores for the "lion" to run after outside.

Sallie and Lallie and Buddy thought England was quite an exciting sort of place! They would have liked to stay much longer at the nice white cottage with the thatched roof, but there were other things they had to see.

When the day came for them to leave Uncle Tom gave Milly-Molly-Mandy a real dollar bill – to use when she came to visit America one day, he said.

Milly-Molly-Mandy is keeping it safe in her treasure-box.

20

MILLY-MOLLY-MANDY
GOES SLEDGING

ONCE UPON A TIME, one cold grey wintry day, Milly-Molly-Mandy and the others were coming home from school.

It was such a cold wintry day that everybody turned up their coat-collars and put their hands in their pockets, and such a grey wintry day that it seemed almost dark already, though it was only four o'clock.

"Oooh! isn't it a cold grey wintry day!" said Milly-Molly-Mandy.

"Perhaps it's going to snow," said little-friend-Susan.

"Hope it does," said Billy Blunt. "I'm going to make a sledge."

Whereupon Milly-Molly-Mandy and little-friend-Susan said both together: "Ooh! will you give us a ride on it?"

"Haven't made it yet," said Billy Blunt. "But I've got an old wooden box I can make it of."

Then he said goodbye and went in at the side gate by the corn-shop where he lived. And Milly-Molly-Mandy and little-friend-Susan ran together along the road to the Moggs's cottage, where little-friend-Susan lived. And then Milly-Molly-Mandy went on alone to the nice white cottage with the thatched roof, where Toby the dog came capering out to welcome her home.

It felt so nice and warm in the kitchen, and it smelled so nice and warm too, that Milly-Molly-Mandy was quite glad to be in.

"Here she comes!" said Grandma, putting the well-filled toast-rack on the table.

"There you are!" said Aunty, breaking open hot scones and buttering them on a plate.

"Just in time, Milly-Molly-Mandy!" said Mother, pouring boiling water into the teapot. "Call the men-folk in to tea, but don't keep the door open long."

So Milly-Molly-Mandy called, and Father and Grandpa and Uncle soon came in, rubbing their hands, very pleased to get back into the warm again.

"Ah! Nicer indoors than out," said Grandpa.

"There's snow in the air," said Uncle.

"Shouldn't wonder if we had a fall before morning," said Father.

"Billy Blunt's going to make a sledge, and he *might* let Susan and me have a ride, if it snows," said Milly-Molly-Mandy. And she wished very much that it would.

That set Father and Uncle talking during tea of the fun they used to have in their young days sledging down Crocker's Hill.

Milly-Molly-Mandy did wish it would snow soon.

The next day was Saturday, and there was no school, which always made it feel different when you woke up in the morning. But all the same Milly-Molly-Mandy thought something about her little bedroom looked different somehow, when she opened her eyes.

"Milly-Molly-Mandy!" called Mother up the stairs, as she did every morning.

"Yoo-oo!" called Milly-Molly-Mandy, to show she was awake.

"Have you looked out of your window yet?" called Mother.

"No, Mother," called Milly-Molly-Mandy, sitting up in bed. "Why?"

"You look," said Mother. "And hurry up with your dressing." And she went downstairs to the kitchen to get the breakfast.

So Milly-Molly-Mandy jumped out of bed and looked.

"Oh!" she said, staring. "Oh-h!"

For everything outside her little low window was white as white could be, except the sky, which was dark, dirty grey and criss-crossed all over with snowflakes flying down.

"Oh-h-h!" said Milly-Molly-Mandy again.

213

And then she set to work washing and dressing in a great hurry (and wasn't it cold!) and she rushed downstairs.

She wanted to go out and play at once, almost before she had done breakfast, but Mother said there was plenty of time to clear up all her porridge, for she mustn't go out until the snow stopped falling.

Milly-Molly-Mandy hoped it would be quick and stop. She wanted to see little-friend-Susan, and to find out if Billy Blunt had begun making his sledge.

But Father said, the deeper the snow the better for sledging. So then Milly-Molly-Mandy didn't know whether she most wished it to snow or to stop snowing!

"Well," said Mother, "it looks as if it means to go on snowing for some while yet, so I should wish for that if I were you! Suppose you be Jemima-Jane and help me to make the cakes this morning, as you can't go out."

So Milly-Molly-Mandy tied on an apron and became Jemima-Jane. And she washed up the breakfast things and put them away; and fetched whatever Mother wanted for

cake-making from the larder and the cupboard, and picked over the sultanas (which was a nice job, as Jemima-Jane was allowed to eat as many sultanas as she had fingers on both hands, but not one more), and she beat the eggs in a basin, and stirred the cake-mixture in the bowl. And after Mother had filled the cake tins Jemima-Jane was allowed to put the scrapings into her own little patty-pan and bake it for her own self in the oven (and that sort of cake always tastes nicer than any other sort, only there's never enough of it!)

Well, it snowed and it snowed all day. Milly-Molly-Mandy kept running to the windows to look, but it didn't stop once. When Father and Grandpa and Uncle had to go out (to see after the cows and the pony and the chickens) they came back looking like snowmen.

"Is it good for sledging yet, Father?" asked Milly-Molly-Mandy.

"Getting better every minute, Milly-Molly-Mandy, that's certain," answered Father, stamping snow off his boots on the door-mat.

"I wonder what Susan thinks of it, and if Billy has nearly made his sledge yet," said Milly-Molly-Mandy.

But it didn't stop snowing before dark, so she couldn't find out that day.

The next day, Sunday, the snow had stopped falling, and it looked beautiful, spread out all over everything. Father and Mother and Grandpa and Uncle and Aunty and Milly-Molly-Mandy put on their Wellington boots, or goloshes (Milly-Molly-Mandy had boots), and walked to Church. (Grandma didn't like walking in the snow, so she stayed at home to look after the fire and put the potatoes on.)

Billy Blunt was there with his father and mother, so afterwards in the lane Milly-Molly-

Mandy asked him, "Have you made your sledge yet?"

And Billy Blunt said, "'Tisn't finished. Dad's going to help me with it this afternoon. I'll be trying it out before school to-morrow, probably."

Milly-Molly-Mandy was sorry it wasn't done yet. But anyhow she and little-friend-Susan had a grand time all that afternoon, making a snowman in the Moggs's front garden.

On Monday Milly-Molly-Mandy was in a great hurry to finish her breakfast and be off very early to school.

She didn't have long to wait for little-friend-Susan either, and together they trudged along through the snow. It was quite hard going, for sometimes it was almost over the tops of their boots. (But they didn't always keep to the road!)

When they came to the village there, just outside the corn-shop, was Billy Blunt's new sledge. And while they were looking at it Billy Blunt came out at the side gate.

"Hullo," he said. "Thought you weren't coming."

"Hullo, Billy. Isn't that a beauty! Have you been on it yet? Can we have a ride?"

"You'll have to hurry, then," said Billy Blunt, picking up the string. "I've been up on the hill by Crocker's Farm, past the crossroads."

"I know," said Milly-Molly-Mandy, "near where that little girl Bunchy and her grand-mother live. Can we go there now?"

"Hurry up, then," said Billy Blunt.

So they all hurried up, through the village, past the crossroads and the school, along the road to Crocker's Hill, shuffling through the snow, dragging the sledge behind them.

"Isn't it deep here!" panted Milly-Molly-Mandy. "This is the way Bunchy comes to school every day. I wonder how she'll manage today. She isn't very big."

"We've come uphill a long way," panted little-friend-Susan. "Can't we sit on the sledge and go down now?"

"Oh, let's get to the top of the hill first," panted Milly-Molly-Mandy.

"There's a steep bit there. You get a good run," said Billy Blunt. "I've done it six times. I went up before breakfast."

"I wish I'd come too!" said Milly-Molly-Mandy.

"Sledge only holds one," said Billy Blunt.

"Oh!" said Milly-Molly-Mandy.

"Oh!" said little-friend-Susan.

They hadn't thought of that.

"Which of us has first go?" said little-friend-Susan.

"Don't suppose there'll be time for more than one of you, anyhow," said Billy Blunt. "We've got to get back."

"You have first go," said Milly-Molly-Mandy to little-friend-Susan.

"No, you have first go," said little-friend-Susan to Milly-Molly-Mandy.

"Better hurry," said Billy Blunt. "You'll be late for school."

They struggled on up the last steep bit of the hill.

And there were the little girl Bunchy and her grandmother, hand-in-hand, struggling up it through the snow from the other side. The little cottage where they lived could be seen down below, with their two sets of footprints leading up from it.

"Hullo, Bunchy," said Milly-Molly-Mandy.

"Oh! Hullo, Milly-Molly-Mandy," said Bunchy.

And Bunchy and her grandmother both looked very pleased to see them all. Grandmother had just been thinking she would have to take Bunchy all the way to school today.

But Milly-Molly-Mandy said, "I'll take care of her." And she took hold of Bunchy's little cold hand with her warm one (it was very warm indeed with pulling the sledge up the

221

hill). "You go down in the sledge, Susan, and I'll look after Bunchy."

"No," said little-friend-Susan. "You wanted it just as much."

"Sit *her* on it," said Billy Blunt, pointing to Bunchy. "We can run her to school in no time. Come on."

So Bunchy had the ride, with Billy Blunt to guide the sledge and Milly-Molly-Mandy and little-friend-Susan to keep her safe on it. And Grandmother stood and watched them all go shouting down the steep bit. And then, as Bunchy was quite light and the road was a bit downhill most of the way, they pulled her along easily, right up to the school gate, in good time for school.

And Bunchy *did* enjoy her ride. She thought it was the excitingest thing that had ever happened!

And then after afternoon school (Bunchy had her dinner at school because it was too far for her to go home for it) Billy Blunt told her to get on his sledge again. And he and Milly-Molly-Mandy and little-friend-Susan pulled her all the way home (except up the steepest bit). And

Grandmother was so grateful to them that she gave them each a warm currant bun.

And then Milly-Molly-Mandy and little-friend-Susan took turns riding down the hill on Billy Blunt's sledge. It went like the wind, so that you had to shriek like anything, and your cap blew off, and you felt you could go on for ever! And then, *Whoosh!* you landed sprawling in the snow just where the road turned near the bottom.

Milly-Molly-Mandy and little-friend-Susan each got tipped out there. But when Billy Blunt had gone back to the top of the hill with the sledge for his turn he came sailing down and rounded the bend like a bird, and went on and on and was almost at the crossroads when the others caught him up. (But then, he'd had plenty of practice, and nobody had seen him spill out at his first try!)

It seemed a long walk home to the nice white cottage with the thatched roof after all that, and Milly-Molly-Mandy was quite late for tea. But Father and Mother and Grandpa and Grandma and Uncle and Aunty weren't a bit cross, because they guessed what she had been up to, and of course, you can't go sledging every day!

In fact, it rained that very night, and next day the snow was nearly gone. So wasn't it a good thing that Billy Blunt had got his sledge made in time?

Leabharlanna Poibli Chathair Bhaile Átha Cliath
Dublin City Public Libraries